Andy Pappenfuss

WITHDRAWN

Meeting at the Merry Fifer

MEETING
at the
MERRY FIFER

Merle Constiner

W · W · NORTON & COMPANY · INC · NEW YORK

To Susannah

Meeting at the Merry Fifer

I

THE GRUBBY little tavern, with its weathered sign, "The Merry Fifer," crouched back from the roadside among giant oaks in a cave of vines. For a week Hugh Perrine had been longing for a cup of coffee in a low-grade tavern. You could bring your own food in with you and eat it. Yet he hesitated. He was carrying his life savings, nine dollars.

He was fifteen years old, deep chested and strong, dressed in worn chocolate-brown homespun and stiff workshoes. He had been walking, walking, and there was much more walking ahead of him, but this autumn of 1846 in southern Indiana was particularly beautiful in crystal mauves and fiery crimsons. He was bound for Cincinnati. He had left the small farm, at first heading south. Now he had reached the southern edge of the state and was moving east. Corydon was behind him, and New Albany, and Jeffersonville. This was a wild road, hidden in forest and brush and undergrowth, but an important one, with much dusty traffic. A man in an apron came to the inn door, stared at him, and moved back. A ground hog in its burrow.

Hugh left the road, went up a short walk, and stepped inside. He blinked.

It was, sure enough, a low-grade tavern, all right. Outside, dusk had begun to settle through the trees, and here the gloom was lighted by a single candle on a long, empty table. At another smaller table in a back corner, a shadowed figure ate in silence, bent low over a bowl of thick soup. The innkeeper, a runty, evil-looking man, sat on a stool by the fireplace, drawing a duck on his lap and tossing the viscera on the hearthstone, where they were devoured by a voracious tortoise tomcat. No one paid Hugh the slightest attention as he came in.

He sat at the long table on which the candle stood. He carried a canvas pouch, his only luggage, from a thong over his shoulder. Removing this now and opening it, he laid out on the table before him a heel of bread and two hard-boiled eggs. Up to now, he had done all his eating and his frugal cooking along roadsides, alone, traveling as cheaply as he could.

The innkeeper rose, came over, and stood before him. "A cup of coffee," said Hugh. "Please."

The innkeeper left the room by a door near the fireplace and returned with coffee in a small tin basin. He also held a cube of gingerbread in his stubby fingers. Wordlessly, he placed the basin on the table and shoved out the gingerbread. Why not, Hugh wondered? It looked good. He took it.

It wasn't good, but it was eatable. Twenty minutes later, when he had finished and rested a bit and put the pouch-thong again over his shoulder, he called for his bill.

Once more the innkeeper was standing before him.

"Two dollars," he said.

It was an instant before Hugh could speak.

Outraged, hoarse with anger, he said, "No, sir. You mighty well know I'm not going to pay any two dollars."

"You're going to pay it," said the innkeeper pleasantly, "because I set the prices here, and I say so. Unless I miss my guess, you're a migrant farmer, just finished with his fall stint, and with money in his pocket. It won't hurt you. If you give me trouble, it will. An innkeeper couldn't last long if he couldn't handle a defaultin' customer. The money, you'll forget. The other thing, you never will.

11

Take my word on it. And the law will stand behind me."

"Nevertheless and nevertheless," said the figure eating porridge in the shadows, "I don't believe I'd do it."

He got up casually and walked forward and joined them.

Though at first Hugh thought him to be in his twenties, he finally decided the young man could be his own age, maybe even younger. He was dressed in jacket and pants of cheap slate-gray gingham. His pants were stuffed into short cavalry boots that were warped with wear and run-down at the heels. Something, hardship likely, had pinched and furrowed his face, and his eyes were of the palest blue, emotionless—almost blank.

The innkeeper turned to him with scorn. "Pay your bill too, while we're on the subject, and get out of here. I don't cater to trash."

"I don't much like being called trash," said the other thoughtfully. "Not for myself, but for my friends."

With a sneer, the innkeeper asked, "And who might these friends be?"

"I'm a cordwainer, whipping the stump."

Whipping the stump meant that he had served his apprenticeship and was now a journeyman, an itinerant, putting the finishing touches to his trade. Hugh could hardly believe it. He looked so young when you really studied him.

Cordwainer journeymen, the shoemakers, were a rough and ready clan to have set against you.

The innkeeper looked surly, but disturbed.

The stranger handed him five pennies. "For my soup," he said. To Hugh, he said, "Give him a dime."

Hugh did. The innkeeper put the coins in his pocket.

Hugh's new friend said, "Shall we get a little fresh air?"

"Suits me," said Hugh.

Side by side, they left.

They walked together in the dusk, down the road, neither of them saying anything. Finally Hugh said, "If you're a journeyman cobbler, where are your tools? Your workpack?"

"See?" said the other, laughing. "You're smarter than him. I'm no cobbler. How could I be? I'm just two months shy of fifteen, I think. We never kept much track of time in my family."

This, Hugh decided, was right. Fifteen.

"My name's Joe Caffery," the boy said.

"I'm Hugh Perrine. Why did you do it?"

"You would have did it for me."

Surprised, Hugh said, "Why, I believe I would have." Not with the fancy lie, he thought, but somehow.

"I could tell that by looking at you," said Caffery with

certainty. "I could tell you were that kind."

At the bend in the road there was an old moss-covered log and behind it a thicket of young hackberry. "Let's sit down a minute," said the boy in gingham. They sat down.

"I want to thank you," said Hugh, faltering. "Two dollars is a heap of money."

"Then tell me a little about yourself," said Caffery. "I've not had much talk in the last few days, and I'm not likely to for some time to come."

"There's not much to tell," said Hugh. "For the last year I've been an ax-farmer, and that's the hardest kind." An ax-farmer, he explained, took an ax with him into the real bad new ground to plant around tree roots and such. He had worked for a poor man with a family of seven, and when the land finally got going, and they couldn't afford him anymore, they let him go. He had been an orphan for two years. Typhoid had gotten his parents, both with one blow. "It missed me," he said softly, "though there has been times, I admit, when I wisht it hadn't. I guess I'm too mean and tough." He said he was bound for Cincinnati.

He told how hard a sorry-dirt farmer had to labor, burning brush, carting pumpkins for winter feed for stock, fighting a dull shovel plow through dry rocky clay. And whatever you were doing, you were always behind in doing it.

"But you had stuff to eat," said Caffery. "Like crab-apple preserves and dried mush."

"Yes," said Hugh. "Sometimes. That side seemed to slip my mind." He turned to gaze at his companion. "If you're not a journeyman cobbler, then what are you?"

"I'm an indentured boy and a runaway," said Caffery softly, "trying not to get shot, not to get hurt. And with a hunch that they're closing in on me."

Aghast and overcome with concern, Hugh said, "Then what were you doing in a public tavern, you bonehead. You should be deep in the brush!"

"I was," said Caffery. "But I'm no Indian and I got crazy hungry."

Then, abruptly, Hugh realized the great bravery Joe Caffery had displayed at the tavern, how he had come out of obscurity and deliberately confronted the innkeeper for Hugh's sake, making a public scene.

"What is an indentured boy?" Hugh asked quietly. "I mean just what?"

He had heard of indenture all his life, of course, but the custom hadn't existed in the community in which he grew up.

"No matter what else you call it, it's a kind of slavery," said Caffery. "A man needs some cheap help. He looks

around, finds a likely boy, and goes to the boy's parents
or guardian. The man and the boy's guardian draw up a
paper. The paper is called by several names, an indenture,
a contract, or deed. The guardian deeds the boy away
like he was a piece of property."

"Then the man owns the boy?"

"Until he's twenty-one, under the law. Most of these
contracts are all the same, like a bill of sale. They say
what the master, the owner, can or can't do and what the
boy can or can't do. A boy doesn't get paid a penny, for
instance. Any money he makes outside his contract
duties doesn't belong to him. By law, if I hold a horse
for a stranger and get paid one cent, that cent has to be
turned over to my master."

"And he can beat you half to death?"

"If the whim takes him, and he don't have nothing better to do."

"Is that why you ran away, because of a hard master?"

"No. He wasn't really hard, except at times. And any
boy, bound or free, has to look forward to a little of that
at times. It's hard for me to put into words to you, but I
ran away because I want to turn out worthwhile and I
couldn't see any future ahead of me."

"Yes," said Hugh. "Yes." He took a deep breath and
said, "Isn't there any legal way to get out of it?"

16

"I was indentured when I was eleven, over in Illinois. The man, name's Gadsby, give my uncle, my guardian, fifty dollars. My uncle spent it in a month and died. But even if I had fifty dollars to offer him, I doubt if Gadsby would take it and release me."

Hugh, who liked arithmetic, began to figure aloud. "Fifty dollars for ten years service is five dollars a year. And a little over forty-one cents a month, and less than two cents a day. I can see why this Mr. Gadsby wouldn't want to let you go."

They got up. They didn't look at each other.

Hugh took a silver dollar from his pocket. From his pouch, he took his remaining reserve of food, three eggs and a stale cinnamon bun, and pushed them at Caffery.

Caffery took the food. He wouldn't even touch the money.

"Now hit for the brush," Hugh said briskly. "Right now! Get!"

Caffery disappeared into the hackberry thicket.

Hugh, unhappy, stood for a moment, then started down the road. As he walked, he glanced left and right, looking for a good place to spend the night.

There was a big white moon in the sky. Everything was almost like daylight, and walking was easy. It was about ten minutes after he had left Caffery, when he came to the cedar tree.

It was a large bush, really, charcoal black, close to the road, and as he came up to it a man stepped out, confronting him with elbows crooked and hands clenched, ready to grab.

He was a skinny man, wearing a farmer's plush cap, and, probably because the night was turning crisp, a thin black ankle-length coat, so tattered that Hugh could see its rents and curly, ragged ends in the moonlight. His long-jawed face was waxlike.

"You a whippersnapper named Joe Caffery?" he asked.

Hugh came to a stop and said nothing.

He had started to say no, then changed his mind. The longer he could delay, the farther Joe Caffery could go before this man took up the hunt again. He remained silent.

"You don't deny it," said the man, pleased. He looked Hugh over. "You're him all right. Dressed different than I was told, but the right age. So come along. And don't give me any trouble."

They turned from the highway, down an old log road.

"I knew you'd pass," said the man. "Boy-huntin', says I to myself, will be like deer huntin'. Take your stand and wait."

"You an officer of the law?" asked Hugh.

"No," said the man. "But I'd be a dandy, wouldn't I?" He sounded flattered. "I'm jest an honest tiller of the earth that always enjoys a little huntin' or trappin'."

Almost immediately, the road came out into a saucer-shaped clearing, ringed by practically leafless black trees twisted against the bright-blue night sky. The turf was spongy and luxuriant underfoot. Through the center of the hollow ran a shallow creek, spotted with flat stones that were pale white in the moonlight. On the far perimeter, to the left, was a small campfire with a man sitting by it. Three indistinct horses were tethered nearby, grazing. In the center of the hollow, at the stream's edge, was a second, much larger campfire, and beside it, a sort of wagon Hugh had seen many times. It was a peddler's wagon, and a big one. A great draylike body, maybe seven feet long and six high, with a driver's seat in front, was set on four heavy wheels. A man was sitting by the fire there, splicing a rope. It was to this fire and man that Hugh's captor led him.

The man got up as they joined him.

He was a florid, bulbous middle-sized man, with pop-eyes that seemed moist in the firelight. He was dressed in wrinkled black wool and wore side-laced canvas leggings that came up to his knees.

Hugh's captor, the farmer, said, "Well, here he is,

Mr. Gadsby. He gave me a heck of a fight, but I subdued him. The word you put out was that you was offering a handsome reward for his return. How much?"

Hugh stepped forward. This is the moment, he thought. When he heard no word of contradiction, Hugh was stunned.

Gadsby stuck his huge face into Hugh's and said, "Well, Joe, how does it feel to be back? Have a nice vacation?"

At first it made no sense to Hugh. And then it did. Gadsby wanted a boy. And any boy, any boy at all, would do. Hugh thought it over. What if he could give Joe Caffery a whole night's head start? And what, when you came right down to it, was there to be afraid of here? What harm could come to him in this little clearing?

To the farmer, Gadsby said, "You heard him. He didn't deny he was my bondboy, did he?"

"How could he?" said the farmer. "I caught him, didn't I?"

"I just wanted you to be a witness," said Gadsby.

Now, suddenly, Hugh was scared. What chance would he have in a backcountry court with Gadsby and the farmer swearing against him? When you looked at it that way, then, right now, this very minute, he was as good as indentured himself.

Tomorrow he would simply vanish, he decided. If Caffery could do it, he could do it.

"Now, if you please," said the farmer. "I'll take my money and go."

"The handsome reward isn't money," said Gadsby. "It's better than money."

The farmer looked bewildered. "Better than money?"

"Yes," said Gadsby. He unbuttoned his jacket and un-hooked a big yellow watch from his watch chain. Hand-ing the watch to the farmer, he said somberly, "Twenty-two carat. It belonged to my late beloved father, and I prize it far higher than filthy lucre."

"Well, thanks," said the farmer, impressed. "I hate to admit it, but I've never owned a watch." He put it in his pocket.

"If it stops ticking," said Gadsby, "shake it gently. Good watches are sensitive. If it won't start, try, try again."

The farmer nodded and left the clearing.

Gadsby went to the wagon and came back to the fire with a satchel. When he opened it and took out a big yellow watch, Hugh saw that the bag was filled with sim-ilar watches. "Brass," said Gadsby proudly but confi-dentially. "Hardly more than trinkets. I buy them by the quarter gross." Hanging the replacement on his chain, he

21

said, "You haven't said a word. Can't you talk at all, son?"

"Yes," said Hugh, "when I choose to." He lapsed back into silence.

Gadsby, enjoying himself, kept up the pretense, saying, "And, Mr. Caffery, what name did you go by whilst you was away?"

"Hugh Perinne."

"Would you like me to call you that from now on?"

"I don't much care."

Gadsby went to his wagon, took its whip from the socket by the front seat and snapped it limberly in the air a few times.

He said, "When a bondboy transgresses, his master has an obligation to chastize him. When he runs away he gets it. When he doesn't respect and adore his master he gets it. When at all times, he doesn't scurry around and sweat blood trying to be a perfect servant he gets it. Are you going to obey all these rules and regulations?"

"I doubt it," said Hugh mildly.

"I feared as much. Fact is, even if you had said yes, it wouldn't have made no difference. I'm going to touch you up a little anyway. Just to point you in the right direction."

"I never liked being hit," said Hugh quietly. "Not by strangers."

A soft, relaxed, pleasant whistling came to their ears. They turned. A man was walking slowly toward them from the campfire at the other side of the clearing. Smiling, he stepped into the rim of firelight. "Good evening," he said amiably. "What's the whip for?"

He was a tall lean man in his middle thirties, perhaps, dressed in a suit of modest mixed tweed; his waistcoat was low cut, and his shirt front ruffled. He wore Wellington boots that had been waxed until they looked varnished. His face was lean and muscled and somber, and his hand, when he brought his pipe to his lips, was long, narrow, and sinewy. The pipe was a large meerschaum, carved with racing, jumping, and galloping horses.

"I'll thank you to mind your business," said Gadsby, making his face ugly.

The man took a casual puff from his pipe. "And I'll thank you to talk civilly, or I'll put the popper of that whip where it belongs."

Gadsby's manner changed. Placatingly, he said, "This boy is bound to me. He run away. I just got him back. I'm fixing to take the reward money out of his hide. It's perfectly normal and customary."

Addressing Hugh, the man said, "I'm Dan Nichols. Who are you?"

Hugh gave him that blank, wordless stare. It was hard

23

not to answer him; he liked him, but this was no time to upset the applecart.

"His name is Joe Caffery," said Gadsby. "And I've got the paper to prove it."

"Is that right?" asked Nichols. "And did you run away?"

Hugh simply looked at him.

After a moment of meditation, Nichols said, "There's something about this I don't care for. Could I see that contract?"

Gadsby unlocked the back of the wagon, rummaged in a strongbox, and came out with a folded sheet of paper. Nichols held it close to the dying fire and studied it.

After an interval he read, " 'Master herein agrees to instruct boy adequately in schoolwork.' Do a problem for me."

Hugh said, "If a boy is indentured for ten years for fifty dollars, he's working for a little over forty-one cents a month."

Nichols grinned. "Next. 'Master must supply boy with appropriate food and clothes.' Satisfied with your clothes?"

"Yes," said Hugh.

"Decent food?"

"No complaint," said Hugh, "so far."

Nichols returned the document to Gadsby. "I still don't like it," he said. "There's something here I can't put my finger on. Get rid of that whip." Gadsby returned it to its socket near the wagon seat.

Nichols said goodnight and left them.

When they were alone, Hugh said gently, "Maybe we'd better get this over with. I'd like to know just how we stand."

Gadsby looked startled. "Found your voice, hey?" he said. "Well, here's how we stand. I think you and me will get along all right, but naturally we'll have to wait and see. Time will tell. At first you was a puzzle to me, but I think I've got you solved. You allowed yourself to be took and come along peaceful, because you was homeless and hungry. Am I right?"

"Everybody gets hungry some time or other," said Hugh blandly.

"Yes," said Gadsby. "That's the truth. And they ain't no shame in it. Now you just be a good boy, and helpful, and your troubles are over. Care for a little bite of grub before you go to bed?"

"I can wait until breakfast."

"See? You're starting off right. Polite and humble. I'll

25

sleep here by the ashes, and you can bed down there under the wagon."

Next morning, first thing, as soon as Hugh opened his eyes, he looked across the clearing. Dan Nichols and his three horses were gone.

II

GADSBY WAS SITTING at the fire, tending a big skillet of
bacon and eggs, with an enamel coffee pot nudged into
the embers at his side when Hugh crawled out from
under the wagon bed. Gadsby called out a cheery good
morning and Hugh, surprised at this sudden good nature,
answered cautiously in a not unfriendly manner. He
went to the creek and took out his toothbrush, two inches
of althea twig which he had carefully chewed to a frayed
end in the backcountry custom and gave his strong
teeth a hardy scrubbing. He then threw cold water on
his face and neck.

He went to the campfire, sat on his haunches across

from Gadsby, and looked things over. The boxlike structure on the wagonwheels, the "store," was makeshift and delapidated, but big. On its top was lashed a willow-withe chicken crate. A big mean-looking rooster was tied by its leg with a length of fishline to a wagon spoke. It was lustrous gray with long glossy feathers. A gamecock. A fine one, too, tall and commanding in its manner.

"Admiring my chicken?" asked Gadsby, pleased. "That's a Virginia Gray, if you don't know about 'em. They ain't no better strain. It's sometimes called a strychnine."

"You fight chickens?" asked Hugh.

"This one's a pet," said Gadsby shortly. "Help yourself to the skillet."

"Which direction are we headed?" asked Hugh.

"East."

East was Hugh's direction. He made up his mind to stay on a little longer. Why not travel with Gadsby? He would have food and a place to sleep. He could always slip away when he wanted.

Gadsby said, "Before you come to me, was you bound or free? You don't have to answer that one unless you want to."

"I was free," said Hugh.

"Maybe yes, maybe no," said Gadsby. "But I'll tell

28

you one thing. They's enough runaway boys these days to sail a hundred clipper ships to China."

"This is good bacon," said Hugh.

"I traded a farmer a tin dipper for a side of it."

"That was a thievin' thing to do," said Hugh.

"It's all in how you look at it," said Gadsby. "The farmer needed the dipper bad, and I needed the bacon. Both of us was satisfied. And there's this, too. In a week my bacon will be gone, and twenty years from now the farmer will still have his dipper. One thing you'd better get through your head right now," he continued with a sudden underlay of menace, "is that I set the morals in this corporation. When I want your opinion on anything, I'll say so. And this is as good a time as any to tell you your duties."

In camp Gadsby would do the cooking, but Hugh would lay things out and clean things up afterward. He was to tend and groom the horse and feed the chicken twice a day, morning and night. At those times when the store was in operation, Hugh was to stand by, alert, ready to obey the slightest lifting of Gadsby's finger. Menial tasks of any nature categorically were Hugh's job.

"But most of all," said Gadsby, "be careful what you say, which won't be no great difficulty for you. Not only when I'm selling, but in camp."

"In camp?" said Hugh. "You mean when just the two of us are alone?"

"They'll be times when we won't be alone," said Gadsby. "They'll be times, like now, when we put into a peddlers' camp."

"Is this a peddlers' camp?"

"So to speak. These days the highways and byways, roads and back roads has its own moving, itinerant, riding and walking life. It's own world, you might say—peddlers and journeymen, acrobats and clock-menders, dancing masters and tricksters, and dozens of others. All over this country, east of the Mississippi, there's a sort of network of places when they choose to camp, where it's unlikely they'll be sharing their supper with a sheriff."

While Hugh pondered this, Gadsby said, "Wash up the plates, and harness up the horse. We better get on the pike."

As Hugh rose, Gadsby said, "I'll put away the chicken. Always. Or he'll take out your eyes with those spurs."

With Gadsby holding the reins and Hugh beside him on the high seat, they drove out the log road and turned east on the pike. They rode for a while across a soft, resilient blanket of scarlet leaves, dropped by the frost, and, after a bit, left the forest and came out into an area of unprosperous-looking farming country. It was about nine o'clock when they came to the first residence, a log cabin with a clapboard roof, set back behind a yard of tree stumps. A frog-faced middle-aged woman in linsey sat on the cedar-log doorstep, sunning herself in the pleasant morning and peeling apples for drying. Nearby played two children, a boy of seven, perhaps, and a girl of twelve. Gadsby said, "She's too young to be their grandmother, I'd say. That means, if they're hers, that they came to her sort of late in life. That means she treasures them."

He turned from the road and pulled in about twelve feet from the woman.

She said, "Just move on along. We don't need anything."

"Get down," said Gadsby. Hugh and Gadsby got to the ground.

Gadsby unlocked both sides of the wagon. Each side had a pair of large swinging doors hinged at the far corners. When Hugh gazed at the wares confronting him on his side, he blinked. There were shelves and racks and hanging things, glinting and immaculate—just about everything you could think of—lace, spices and essences, pottery, razors, scissors, hats, boots, firearms. And tinware! tin ovens, graters, colanders, kettles, pots, and pans. Everything.

The children came up to the store; and soon the woman came also.

Pretending to ignore them, Gadsby produced a spool of scintillating ribbon, silver and green. Deftly, almost before anyone realized it, he picked up scissors, cut off a length of the ribbon, and wrapped it like a bandeau around the girl's long hair. In the same flowing motion, before she could gasp with joy, he put a tin whistle in the little boy's pudgy hand.

The woman smiled faintly, grudgingly. "Well," she said, "I guess I could use a colander. How much are they?"

"Twenty cents," said Gadsby. "And they're top notch."

He took one down and handed it to her. "Anything else? I may never be through here again."

"That'll be all," she said. She took the money out of a little breast pocket.

Gadsby looked at it as though he couldn't quite understand it. "Forty-five cents," he said. "Twenty cents for the ribbon, five for the whistle, and twenty for the colander."

The woman's face went an angry red. "I thought the ribbon and whistle were gifts."

32

Gadsby looked sad. "And who, madam, gives me gifts?"

To the children, the woman said severely, "Return them."

The little boy began to cry. The girl looked heart-broken.

"Oh, keep them," said the woman. To Gadsby, she said in a rage, "But now I don't want your colander." She added five cents to the coins in her hand, and poked them at Gadsby. He didn't take them.

"I want to leave no hard feelings behind me," he said. "I may be through here again." He took down a tin coffee-pot. "Coffeepot, plus ribbon, plus whistle, plus colander, eighty-five cents?"

She shook her head. "Get off my land."

Gadsby took the twenty-five cents from her open palm, locked the wings of his cart, and lifted his finger to Hugh. They climbed to the wagon seat, and Gadsby drove off.

About a half-mile down the pike, Hugh said, "Do you call that good business?"

"Very good. Three hundred percent profit on that cheap ribbon, and four hundred percent on the boy's whistle."

"But only twenty-five cents."

"Don't worry about the totals; just worry about the

percentages. Somebody else will buy that colander. Don't worry about that. We didn't destroy it, you know. We just put it back on the shelf."

"Were you really going to take that ribbon from the girl?"

"Yes, indeed. Twenty cents."

"I felt sorry for her."

Gadsby snapped the reins. "Oh, you'll get over that."

Hugh looked uncomfortable.

Gadsby said, "Look at it this way. An hour ago, those children had nothing. Now they have a whistle and a ribbon and are as happy as skylarks."

"Like the farmer who gave a side of bacon for a cheap dipper."

"Now you're getting the idea."

So it went from then on, stop after stop, with Gadsby, glib, quick, changing his approach, adapting himself nimbly to any situation they might encounter. If there was anything honest about Gadsby, Hugh couldn't discover it. He could be friendly, and for a moment you liked him, or he could be cruel in a flash. But there was no doubt about it. He was utterly selfish, and if he had a heart at all it was of stone.

Late in the afternoon, they came to a crossroads, or a fork, really, where a rocky road at their left snaked down from a clump of timbered hills and ended at a lonesome blacksmith's shop.

Adjoining the shop along the pike was a level pasture, now with dry grass. Here five young men in their middle twenties, maybe, were having an athletic contest. Gadsby said, "I've always liked sports. Would you like to watch it for a while?"

Hugh, already entranced, said, "That would be fine."

They were young backwoodsmen, Hugh could tell at a glance, and pretty good. He watched them with pleasure, and yet uneasily. It was a mean, noisy pack, he decided, and a good place to find bad trouble. They constantly broke off their play to quarrel with and curse one another. The leader of the pack was a gangling, stubble-faced man with a chin coated by tobacco juice. He looked like as much poison as all the others put together.

He won every event. They lifted anvils. They raced. They jumped. They threw the maul and pitched the crow-bar: all sports that Hugh himself had engaged in. And always the gangling man won. Sometimes, it looked to Hugh, he won because he seemed to be really best, as in the maul-pitching. Sometimes, as in the foot race, it seemed a little as though he won because he scared his competitors.

When things took a lull and the men were standing in

35

a group, getting their breath back, Gadsby raised his voice and called to them. "Any of you gentlemen named Clyde Holloway?"

They turned and stared.

In a low voice Hugh said, "Who is Clyde Holloway?"

In an equally low voice Gadsby said, "How do I know? I just made it up."

The men came forward and stood in a knot by the wagon seat.

The leader of the pack said with animal curiosity, "What do you want with him?"

"I'm Monongahela Jones," said Gadsby. "I got a parcel for him. A friend of mine, a gunsmith in Cincinnati, knowing that I was coming through here, asked me to deliver it."

"What kind of a parcel?" asked the gangling bully.

"A gun."

"Let's have a look at it."

Gadsby descended to the ground. From under the wagon seat, he took a longish object wrapped in bed ticking. He unwrapped it. The men crowded around him.

The long object was a Kentucky rifle with about a forty-six-inch barrel, Hugh decided. The gun, a little old looking, had once been a flintlock but had recently been converted to a percussion cap. The caplock was new and gleaming, and you could tell it had just been put on. The leader of the pack took it from Gadsby and examined it.

On the metal by the breech, very faintly, you could read where it had been stamped, "Brenner."

Brenner, Hugh knew, was famous as a master gunsmith, along with Hawkins and Golcher.

"I don't know who that Brenner was," said Gadsby. "It must be someone or other who owned it before Mr. Holloway."

The men exchanged wooden glances.

"You selling this to Holloway?" asked the bully.

"Oh, no," said Gadsby. "It's his. He already owns it. I'm just supposed to collect the small amount he owes the man in Cincinnati for putting on the new percussion lock."

"You're in luck," said the bully. "This Holloway happens to be next neighbor to me." His friends cast down their eyes slyly. "I'll just pay for the new lock myself and deliver the gun to him, and he can make it right."

"Not too much trouble?" asked Gadsby.

"No trouble at all. A pleasure. How much?"

"Five dollars and fifty cents," said Gadsby carelessly.

Popeyed, the bully said, "I don't call that no small amount!" He wet his lips avidly. "I jest don't have that much on me."

Regretfully, Gadsby shook his head and started to re-wrap the weapon.

The man said desperately, "I got three dollars and a quarter that I was saving for a trapline."

Gadsby looked interested. "Maybe we could start with that and build it up a little. Maybe your friends would help you out."

They didn't like it, but they did it. They finally got together the five fifty.

The exchange was made, gun for money, and Gadsby mounted the seat and took up the reins. "I hope Mr. Holloway is satisfied with it," he called.

"I guarantee it!" yelled the man.

As they drove away, they left behind them a cluster of scornful, derisive faces.

Out on the pike again, Hugh said, "The gun was no good, eh?"

"It was trash. You can swap them like that out of any city secondhand store for almost nothing. I put on the cheap caplock myself. Expense a dollar thirty."

"Mr. Brenner, if he's still alive, wouldn't like to hear you call a gun of his trash."

"Mr. Brenner never saw that gun. It's a shoddy weapon made years ago for the Indian fur trade."

"How'd his name get on it?" Hugh asked.

"If you got an alphabetical set of dies, like I have, for stamping metal, you could stamp 'em the 'Queen o' Sheba' if they happened to fancy her as a gunsmith," Gadsby boasted.

That evening they camped where night caught them, in a schoolyard. Because of its well, Gadsby explained. Hugh performed his duties. He got out the supper things and drew and brought water. While Gadsby was getting the meal, Hugh groomed the cumbersome old horse. He fed the gamecock.

When they had finished eating, Gadsby allowed the cock to exercise a little, then returned it to its crate. As he sat with Hugh near the embers and as night darkened about them, he said, "That Virginia Gray of mine. His name, if you're interested, is Flash."

Hugh nodded.

"I call him Flash," said Gadsby, "because that's the way he hits—like all Virginia Grays—like lightning, with great force."

"Is that so?" said Hugh.

"Each breed and strain has its own kind of strength," said Gadsby. "Tartars, red, black breasts, yellow legs, is knowed for their fierceness. Thompson Whites are small

but good. Claibornes, black and red, are maybe the gam-
est; they never leave the pit, dead or alive, unless you
take them out. They have big heavy breasts and big low-
hanging wings. The Marksman is a sure hitter, slow
blooded, but stubborn. Tilt Hammers are big and powerful, heavy and persistent hitters, and have blue eyes, by
the way."

Hugh only half-listened. He was deciding to stay with
Gadsby a day or two longer. The longer, the better for
Caffery.

And when you came right down to it, Gadsby's food
was a lot better than his own.

"A game's eyes tell a lot in themselves," said Gadsby.
"A red eye, in the sport, is known as a ferret eye. Pale yellow is a daw eye. Dark brown is a sloe eye. A good cock
should crow shrill and clear. Its feathers should be short
and stiff, and if it's healthy they should be close to its
skin. I mentioned a while back how brave some cocks
are, but brave ain't enough. The cock has to *hit*. And he
has to fight well at the foot, as they say. That means he's
got to be sure to follow up when he's got his enemy in
trouble."

"Has Flash ever fought?" asked Hugh.

"He's took so many money chickens," said Gadsby,
"that now nobody wants to match him."

III

"Now THIS," said Gadsby the next morning as they approached a sizable cluster of buildings straddling the pike, "is Piltonville. You and me must be mighty careful here. It's a hot spot."

He explained to Hugh what he meant. Many towns and villages didn't like peddlers and passed laws to curb them. For one thing, an itinerant coming through drained off a certain amount of custom from the local merchants. For another, there was in the trade an unfortunate group of sharpsters who gave honest men, like Gadsby, a bad name. Hugh smiled at Gadsby's description of himself as one of the "honest men." Towns like this not only had licensing laws, but had a hodgepodge of other ordinances, dormant and trivial, which they could bring out and dust off when they really wanted to harass. Piltonville went the whole hog. It wouldn't even allow showmen.

"Why not showmen?" asked Hugh.

"Shows are amusement," said Gadsby. "If you live in Piltonville and feel in the need of some amusement, you should go to your local merchant and buy a dime's worth of molasses candy. And keep the money in the family."

"It can't be that bad."

"It's worse. It's dangerous for a peddler even to go riding through."

"Then why don't we go around it?"

"Two reasons. First, they ain't no roads north or south. Second, we need matches. Here's the way we'll do it. I'll pull up in front of a store and sit there, looking absent-minded and all-fired innocent. You get down, go in, and buy them. Don't let no trouble start, even if somebody spits in your face."

"I don't think I'd like that," said Hugh.

"They's worse things," said Gadsby. "Leg irons, for instance."

Hugh shot him a quick, skeptical glance, but his face was expressionless.

The business section of the town, when Gadsby pulled alongside the boardwalk and stopped, proved to be composed of two rows of ramshackle shops and offices, sagging and askew, facing each other across a rutted road. Across the street was a public well with a big tin pipe, which could be used, when necessary, to fill the public watering trough adjacent to it. The sides of the watering trough were covered with green slime. Gadsby gave Hugh a coin and said, "All right. Get in and out. Quick."

The store Hugh faced had a tall narrow door with blistered paint. The window to his right was stacked with bolts of bright calico, marked "BARGAIN." The window to his left contained nothing but a spread-out napkin in its center with a sweet potato on it. The sweet potato had grown into a rotting old shoe; a placard beside it said, *"Remarkable curiosity dug up on the Bigsby Walton farm, out at Cherry Forks."* Hugh opened the door and entered.

Just over the threshold, on the floor, lay a half-crumpled handbill. Big black letters on the yellow paper said, "DAN NICHOLS." That much was visible, nothing more.

Hugh picked it up in surprise and carried it with him to the counter. Behind the counter, a crabby-looking man in tin-rimmed spectacles who looked at him with distaste, said, "Yes?"

Hugh spread the handbill out on the counter and read it.

DAN NICHOLS
And
His Three Royal Horses
Fancy Riding
Two and Three Horses
At Full Speed
Perilous Mounting & Dismounting
At Full Speed—Yes
Plus Other Hazardous and Skilled
DISPLAYS OF HORSEMANSHIP

Down at the bottom, Dan had written in red crayon, "Main Street—2:30."

Hugh asked, "Is this today?"

The shopkeeper said sourly, "It's no day. He passed out that bill yesterday morning, and they promptly ordered him to move on. No showmen in Piltonville. What you want?"

When the daze cleared, Hugh said, "Matches. A dime's worth."

When the shopkeeper wrapped them up in a little twist of newspaper and handed them to him, Hugh asked, "Which way did he go?"

"What was that?"

44

"When he left town, which way did he go?"

"I don't know, son. Oh, yes, I do. He came in from the west, and we seen him and his horses leave toward the east. And I have to admit they was mighty nice horses."

As Hugh started to leave, the shopkeeper said, "Wait a minute."

Hugh paused.

"Didn't I see you jest get down from that peddling wagon out there?"

Hugh met the man's eyes squarely and said, "Yes."

"Tell your pa," the storekeeper said coldly, "if he so much as sells a bent pin in this town, the sky is going to fall on him."

"He already knows it," said Hugh. Then, careful to agree, not to seem impudent, not to cause any trouble, he said, "But I'll sure tell him."

"Peddlers is born thieves," said the man. "Are you learning the trade?"

"Not very fast. I'm not very smart."

"My advice is this. Run away."

"Run away?"

"Sure. Learn to beat on a drum and join the army. Live an easy, wholesome life. Have you ever thought that over?"

"No, sir," said Hugh. "But I will. Thank you."

Hugh edged out the door as quickly as he could.

He was two miles out of town before he got his nerves settled.

He didn't mention Dan Nichols to Gadsby.

Piltonville was too good for Dan Nichols. But a wonderful sweet potato growing into a wonderful rotten shoe was just about its style.

That evening, after a surprisingly active and hard day, Gadsby clicked his tongue abruptly at his mare and turned her from the pike into the mouth of a tunnel of high trees, interlaced overhead. For perhaps a half-mile, they followed this leafy road and came out, at last, into a sizable open space, hedged in on all sides by wild shrubbery. At the far edge of the grassy quadrangle, still clearly visible in the early dusk, was an old sawmill, dilapidated and abandoned, the water of its millrace glossy in the twilight. In the center of the quadrangle, three men sat around a big flat campfire. These men were strangers to Hugh. There were no wagons in sight.

Like the first camp, in which Hugh had pretended to go into bond to Gadsby, this place was secretive and hidden.

Gadsby pulled up about twenty feet from the fire and men, got down, and joined them. Hugh unhitched the mare, tethered her, fed the gamecock, and looked around.

46

Taking the coffeepot, he crossed the clearing, located the creek above the mill dam, and got coffee water for supper. Returning with the pot to the wagon, he got out supper food, a big steak and four potatoes, and took them all to the fire.

Careful not to stare at the strangers, he handed the food to Gadsby. Gadsby made coffee, put on the pot, and began to peel potatoes.

Now, trying to appear casual, Hugh began to observe his companions.

A thin man with milk-white hair and skin, a pink-eyed albino dressed in bottle green, sat feeding a small dog pork chops. The dog, a King Charles spaniel with soft eyes and a silken coat, was about the nicest dog that Hugh had ever seen.

Gadsby, putting the potatoes into the skillet alongside the steak, said, "What does your dog do, friend?"

To Hugh, Gadsby said, "He's a tavern showman. Shows in taverns and public squares and places like that."

"What kind of tricks?" asked Hugh.

"Stands on his forepaws, upright on the top of my head, for one thing," said the albino.

"I'd sure like to see him do it," said Hugh.

"You got a penny to throw away?"

Hugh shook his head no.

47

"Then," said the albino, nibbling the chop bone the dog had been eating. "Then, you best forget it. Rex is money crazy."

"Yes, sir," said Hugh. He and the dog gazed at each other affectionately.

Next to the albino sat a misshapen little man in Spanish brown with a battered brown beaver atilt on his head. He was eating nothing; apparently he had nothing to eat. When Hugh glanced at him, he said politely, "Name's Duval." All eyes turned on him and he added, "Hair dresser and dancing master." A heavy walking staff was across his knobby knees.

Now the third man spoke. He was middle aged, tow-headed, and wore baggy, incredibly dusty, alpaca. He was a walker, too, Hugh thought, like the others. On the ground, close to his side where it could be guarded, was a black suitcase, a medical kit, Hugh knew. He had seen these walking doctors back home. In fact it was the only kind he had ever seen.

He cut two slices from a loaf of bread, put a thick slice of boiled ham between them, and handed the sandwich to Duval. "Would you do me the honor of sharing my meal with me?"

This surprised Hugh. He had always heard that hair dressers and dancing masters, too, for that matter, were

48

useless kinds of men.

Duval made a short courteous speech and took the sandwich.

"I've heard that name Duval someplace," said Gadsby. He and Hugh began to eat.

The doctor said, "Who hasn't? Monsieur Duval is from New Orleans. There was a time—before a carriage ran away and he, seeing it, caught a hickory shaft through his shoulder trying valiantly to save its occupants, strangers to him, by the way—that he was one of the country's most famous professional duelists."

"That, I don't understand," said Hugh conversationally. "I don't mean to cause offense, but I always thought dueling was not a commercial proposition. I always thought it was strictly a thing of honor between gentlemen."

"Honor," said the doctor, meeting his eyes. "Can you use a pistol?"

"A rifle, yes. But not a pistol."

"Well, I happen to be a crack shot. If I challenged you in such circumstances you couldn't retreat. Would you call our affair, your murder, a thing of honor?"

"No," said Hugh.

"In the old days, a professional duelist handled such a situation. You went to him with your problem. He took

49

over. He didn't substitute, you understand. He just picked his own little quarrel with the man, and took care of it first, himself."

"I believe in fair play and fair play only," said Monsieur Duval. "I always investigated before I engaged."

"I don't know," said Hugh doubtfully. It still didn't sound very honorable. These men, all of them, were so different from anything he had ever known or even imagined. Even their world and thinking were hard to grasp.

"Well," said the albino in admiration. "There's more than one way to skin a cat even if you're a gentleman, which I'm not."

There was the creaking of an axle, and they all turned. In the indistinct light, they could see only that it was a cart pulling into the clearing. It had a sort of platform bed and a long coffinlike box, drawn by a mule. A man got down. He unhitched the mule and picketed it. He fiddled around. After a bit, they could see he was eating some kind of cold food, probably, alone. Apparently, he didn't want to have to share anything with them.

Finished eating, the man groped about the wagonbed, got hold of something about the size of a hat, and came toward the others and the fire.

As he stepped into the circle of firelight, Hugh saw that he was old, with ropey white hair hanging down from under his hatband and framing his face on either side. He had cold little eyes, a veined nose, a cruel, in-puckered, small mouth. Under his arm, he had a game-cock. The conversation immediately turned on the chicken. There was no preamble. Nobody greeted any-body.

"What do you think of him?" asked the old man. His voice was harsh and rasping.

"I've seen better, and I've seen worse," said Gadsby.

"You a game fancier?" asked the old man.

"I've been so called."

"Not by me," said the old man hatefully. "I never seen you before."

"I'm Charlie Gadsby," said Gadsby. "Small wares. This is Joe Caffery, my apprentice. I've never been on this road before. I just come up from the south."

Standing the cock on the ground and holding it care-fully under the wings, the old man let the group examine it. It was bright red with a black breast and had rattle-snake-colored legs. Gadsby explained it to Hugh, "That's a Susquehanna Red. They is much favored by raftsmen and rivermen. A Susquehanna Red is like a pig in a poke. It may be good, or it may be bad. In my estimation, even when it's good it's only so-so."

In a lucid monotone, the old man said, "Is that a

chicken o' yours in that crate on that wagon?"

"Yes," said Gadsby. "A Virginia Gray."

"Do you fight him, or are you aiming to eat him?"

Gadsby choked with anger. "You don't know what you're getting into," he said. "Don't taunt me, old man."

"Don't call me old man. My name's Greenwood. Would you like to match him for a small wager, say twenty dollars?"

Twenty dollars. Now everyone was staring.

"Yes," said Gadsby. "As soon at I can get him out of his crate. We'll build us up a nice big fire—and watch the slaughter."

"Hold on," said Greenwood. "I fight my cock with a long gaffle. Two-and-a-half inches. Agreed?"

Hugh had once seen a pair of gaffles, ugly, razor-sharp, artificial spurs used in matches.

"Those are a heap longer than mine," said Gadsby, "but I agree. Too long a gaffle encumbers the cock."

"One more question," said Greenwood. "Has your chicken ever fought before?"

"Many times."

"Now this is a warning. Has he always fought picked fights?"

"That's enough of that," said Gadsby. "I'll match him against anything that comes down the road."

"You said it, not me," said the old man, grinning. "Let's seal it before witnesses with a shake."

It was the most unfriendly shaking of hands that Hugh had ever observed.

With his Susquehanna Red under his arm, the old man disappeared in the night toward his cart. The men built up the fire until it was a great roaring crimson bonfire.

Now the old man rejoined them. This time under his arm was not the Red but a muscular, strange-looking chicken that Hugh wouldn't have recognized as a game-cock at all but for its glinting ugly steel gaffles. Its gills and wattles had been removed, making its head look shaved, reptilian. A soft voice by Hugh's shoulder said, "It's been dubbed."

"That's not the Susquehanna," said Gadsby, alarmed. "That's a Shuffler."

"A Shuffler it is," said Greenwood. "But if my memory serves right, you challenged anything that would come along the road. Am I right, gentlemen?"

Nobody liked it. However, everyone but Gadsby and Hugh nodded.

"Get your chicken and its gaffs," said the old man.

Gadsby stood frozen.

In Hugh's ear, Monsieur Duval amplified. "A Shuffler is a madman. Ah, yes. They are not the best fighters, nor the worst. They are what you might call the ruiners. In any fight against any other cock a Shuffler can suddenly turn into a thunderbolt."

Gadsby, jaw hanging, seemed turned to stone.

"That explains the long gaffle," said Monsieur Duval. "This terrible fowl fights wheeling and shuffling and tumbling. Rough and tumble. It strikes its opponent low, for the body, thus the long gaffle. With a short gaffle any cock must strike high, where it can be parried."

In a sepulchral voice Gadsby said, "No."

"What do you mean, no?" said Greenwood. "It's out of your hands now."

"Flash is too old," confessed Gadsby. "I thought one more fight, not too hard, say with that Susquehanna would be all right. But not this. Truth is, he's a pet now."

Hugh, watching Gadsby, knew a strange thing. Gadsby loved, actually loved, that Virginia Gray. He couldn't have believed Gadsby was capable of love at all.

"Then it's a default," said Greenwood.

"That's right," said Gadsby. "Take the credit. I admit it."

"I don't want the credit," said Greenwood. "I want that twenty dollars."

"The old man's right," said the albino. "Fight your cock or pay. A default is the same as a defeat."

"That's the truth," said Greenwood. "And I don't want fifteen, or seven, or a penny less."

Gadsby blustered. "Do you think I'm going to fork over twenty dollars for nothing, nothing at all?"

"You'd better," said the old man malevolently. "Or some night, when you're asleep, somebody is going to burn your wagon. It might not be tonight, and it might not necessarily be me that does it—people can be hired, you know—but I'm giving it to you here and now as a promise."

Gadsby had been staring at him. Gradually into Gadsby's face had come that keen, foxy look that Hugh knew so well.

"Let's step aside here for a minute," said Gadsby, "and talk this over."

They left the group, the others watching them, and went to Gadsby's peddler's wagon. Here they talked for a while. After a bit, Gadsby unlocked the back of the wagon, rummaged around and came out with something or other and a candle which he lit. Now, for a few minutes, he and Greenwood huddled over the candleflame. Finally, they came back to the campfire.

"Mr. Greenwood and I," said Gadsby, "have settled this little proposition with a kind of swap."

It was then that Hugh saw that Greenwood held something in his hand. Joe Caffery's indenture contract.

Gadsby said, "I have made an assignment of interest on the boy's contract to Mr. Greenwood. The default is now settled."

"And," said Greenwood, "on my part, to boot, I've throwed in my Susquehanna Red and the shuffler. How old are you Joe?"

Gadsby said, "Everybody calls him by his nickname, Hugh."

"How old are you, Hugh?"

Dazed, Hugh said, "Fifteen."

"Your indenture runs until you're twenty-one," said Greenwood. "That means you will be with me about six years. You've been eating too much. You're fat."

"That's muscle and bone," said Gadsby. "He's as strong as an ox."

"That's good, because I aim to work him like one," said Greenwood.

It was much later before Hugh learned that an assignment of interest on an indenture was invalid—that if he had been Joe Caffery, which he wasn't, the swap would have been void and illegal. The men were running an enormous bluff, trading on his legal ignorance and certain they could get away with it.

Greenwood was happy with the deal: he would get a

servant free. Gadsby was happy too: his hold on Hugh
was insecure, and he knew it, and he had not only saved
twenty dollars, but also gained a brace of gamecocks.

The others, the albino, the duelist, and the doctor, following the rule of the road, said nothing. The doctor,
however, looked angry.

"Come along, boy," said Greenwood.

They walked across the grass to the mule and the cart
nearby. Now Hugh could see that the big long coffinlike
box on the cart-bed was covered with tarpaulin and
lashed with rope and ringbolts.

"Better get your sleep," said Greenwood, pointing to
the earth. "Tomorrow is a long day. All our days will be
long."

He stood for a moment in the dark before Hugh, and
Hugh could feel, actually feel, the venom in the air.

"If someone should steal twenty dollars and two gamecocks from me," he said at last. "You know what I'd do?
I'd track 'em to the very gates of perdition."

Puzzled, Hugh said, "You mean Mr. Gadsby?"

"I mean you. I mean if you was to run away."

After a moment's silence, Greenwood said, "I'm an old
man with a little nest egg saved up and nothing important
bearing down on me. What I'm trying to say is this. I got
the time, I got the leisure, and I'd do it. I'd sure find you."

If I don't like it, I'll go, thought Hugh. And I'm not going to like it. You can't hold me, and you can't find me. I'll go some time tomorrow.

Joe Caffery is safe by now.

On a whim, Hugh said, "May I ask a question?"

"One and one only. It's a practice I don't care for."

"Which direction are we heading?"

"East."

IV

HUGH WAS AWAKENED by Greenwood's hard boot-toe roughly nudging his ribs. "Get up and hitch," the old man's voice said harshly. "It's time we was on our way."

Dazed with sleep, Hugh hitched. Almost before he was aware of it, he was on the seat, the old man beside him was snapping the reins, the wheels were turning, and they were leaving the camp. A milky, layered fog lay over the clearing. The sky was pitch black; it must be about four o'clock, Hugh thought, observing the stars. The cart passed the fluffy ashes of the fire, and in a circle around it, like lumps of clay, were the sleeping figures of the doctor, the albino, the dancing master, and Gadsby. Soon the cart was on the pike. "When do we generally have break-fast?" asked Hugh.

"We don't have breakfast," said Greenwood curtly. "Breakfast is for loafers and idlers."

The sun was up and well into its climb when they came to the flagpole. It was about thirty feet high, set directly in the middle of the road, with a lantern now extinguished, of course, lashed to it. The road here widened in a big oval to triple its normal width. On their left, as they approached, was a group of buildings, all apparently part of the same establishment: a nice gray frame house, two storied; a gray frame stable behind it; and a scattering of log sheds and out-buildings. Before the house, stretching back from the road, was a large apron of packed dirt like a parade ground, and a few people sat on chairs on the house porch.

In the center of the dirt quadrangle, brightly colored in the sun and empty of passengers, were two stage coaches. Over at one side was a light farm wagon with high narrow wheels and loaded with bales and crates of freight. Greenwood pulled up behind this wagon.

For a moment he sat his seat in silence. Then he said, "If you're going to be my roadboy, you've got to know the road backwards and forwards. What kind of a place is this?"

"A stage stand," said Hugh.

"A *union* stage stand," said Greenwood. "They's a heap difference. Horses are not only kept here and changed, but a union stand caters to several lines. Connections is made here, for one thing. Them two coaches, one a Troy and one a Concord, is so broke down they must be little locals, hopskippers. Their passengers is inside, having a glass of cider and a piece of pie, likely. Locals ain't in no hurry. The really fast coaches, the express coaches, or shake-guts, as they are called, come in like a cyclone, change their horses with the grooms arunnin', and go out like a cyclone. We won't never have no business with a shake-guts on that account."

"The farm wagon just in front of us," said Hugh. "I never saw a farm wagon with wheels like that."

"Some farmer has set himself up in the short distance freightin' business. With them high narrow wheels he can maneuver in any kind of weather. The big wagoners call them sharp-shooters, and do they hate them."

Greenwood got down. "Get off the tarpaulin," he ordered. "I'll be right back. We got to work fast."

He went into the main building. Hugh got down, unlashed the ropes from their ringbolts, took off and folded the tarpaulin. Beneath was a heavy oak box, well mortised and dovetailed.

When Greenwood came back, he was in a rage. "The pig charged me," he snarled. "They're usually glad to have us around. We're an attraction, but he charged me fifty cents. I was a fool to give it. I was a fool to even stop. But maybe we can steal something to even it up before we go."

He opened the box lid and began laying out flannel-wrapped bundles on the platform of the cart-bed.

"This is your first performance," he said viciously. "Up-set it any way and I'll have your ears afterwards. This time, don't do nothing. Oh, yes. They is one thing. When I go around the circle and take up the collection, you follow. Ask everybody in my wake, whether they have already give or not."

Hugh was beginning to get a foggy idea that they were showmen.

"Everybody?" he said.

"You bet, everybody. Sometimes the simple-minded ones has kind hearts and give twice. Sometimes, too, this'll shame the others into finally donating a little."

He began to unwrap the bundles and Hugh watched, fascinated.

Each cloth covering contained a mechanical figure. Some were made of iron, some of iron and wood. They were from a foot to, perhaps, eighteen inches high, and each was on a circular iron base. Fondly, Greenwood arranged them on the cart-bed. As he wound them one by one, he named them to Hugh. "This is the Chinese Princess," he said. She had a knobby iron head with painted eyeballs, long jointed wooden arms, and iron slippers, painted red. Her soiled dress was of lavender chiffon. "This is the Lion of Mysore." The lion was just a lion in a walking posture. Next came a doll in sequins, at the moment on her back, and a funny-looking contraption beside her. "Marie Antoinette and her guillotine." There were four others, but Hugh had no time to observe them. Greenwood had taken up a small accordion and was playing it violently.

The people came down off the porch, people came out of the building, and soon an audience of maybe fifteen had gathered. Among them was a brutish looking man; his red satin waistcoat was gold brocaded, and from the apron at his waist, Hugh deduced that he was the proprietor of the establishment. Behind the proprietor, close to his shoulder in an almost protective stance, stood a hefty stableman with a stupid face.

Subduing his accordion music but keeping up a catchy rhythm, Greenwood began to chant. "You are now about to witness one of the marvels of the age. Genuwine clockwork figures come to this country from faraway Switzerland. The Lion of Mysore." He touched a trigger on the figure, and the lion began to wag his tail, with clicks, and to open and close his jaws with clicks. There was a murmur of approval.

"The Chinese Princess!" yelled Greenwood. The Chinese Princess moved two ways. She circled the perimeter of her disclike base while jerking and contorting her arms and rolling her eyes. As she did these things, Greenwood's accordion fell into a little dance tune, and even to Hugh the illusion was extraordinary.

The show went through its repertoire.

The last figure, the climax, was Marie. "This is Queen Marie Antoinette," bawled Greenwood. "Being beheaded exactly and in every detail as she was so cruelly did by her French subjects."

It was then that Hugh saw a disquieting thing. The man in the apron, the proprietor, was circulating through the crowd with a hat, taking up a collection of his own. And doing very well.

Greenwood placed the sequined doll's neck under the guillotine, placed a tiny grass basket under her head, let fall the guillotine blade; and the rusty iron head, temporarily sealed to the neck with beeswax, dropped gruesomely into the basket.

At this moment, behind him, the proprietor said in a

very loud voice, "Why, thank you, sir. That's exceedingly generous. Thank you."

Greenwood turned. The proprietor, receiving his last donation, was just finishing his round.

The show was over. The crowd dispersed, vanished. The proprietor and his stableman, however, remained.

Frustrated, helpless with rage, Greenwood said, "That is my money."

"Try and get it," said the proprietor icily. His stableman stepped forward. In his hand he had a short stubby hammer. A very ugly fighting instrument, Hugh thought.

The proprietor said coldly, "Get this cart of yours out of my courtyard. This is a busy place, and its space is reserved for paying customers. When outsiders like yourself use it, I usually charge them a small fee, say five cents, but if you get out, and quick, this time I'll forgo it. Move!"

They packed up and left. There was nothing else to do.

As the union stage stand and its flagpole diminished behind them, Greenwood said, "You know what I ought to do?"

Hugh, disturbed by the remark, stiffened. He thought that Greenwood was going to say go back and steal something, maybe at night. He had already shown that his mind was running along those lines. Hugh didn't want

65

to be involved, even indirectly, in anything like that.

Worried, he said, "What?"

"I ought to take you back into a lonesome clump of brush and beat you half to death. And maybe I will. I can't make up my mind."

"But why?" asked Hugh, amazed. "What did I do?"

"It's what you didn't do. You didn't obey orders. You didn't take up that collection, like I precisely instructed you."

"You said follow around after you. You didn't do anything, so I didn't do anything."

"Watch that tongue," grated the old man. "Don't drive me out of control."

They lapsed into silence.

Eleven o'clock went by and twelve and one. This was a barren stretch of road with no taverns and few roadside houses.

When Hugh could stand his hunger no longer, he said, "When do we next eat?"

"Well," said Greenwood wolfishly. "You'll be fixin' me a cup of tea and cutting me a slice of bread in about a hour. Then, at bedtime, you'll be serving me my customary handsome supper. Maybe you'll be eating sometime tomorrow. I can't just say for sure. A starving boy can be a mighty good boy."

A drizzling rain began to fall. From under the seat, the old man took out a stiff oilskin waterproof and put it on. Hugh had no waterproof. Though it was early afternoon, the countryside darkened and became gray. Moisture beaded the bare branches of roadside trees. It became cold. Hugh's jacket became soggy and occasionally, convulsively, surprising him, his teeth threw off a little spasm of chattering.

At about one thirty they came to a primitive log church along the road, empty now. As they approached, they could see behind it a crude shelter, a roof supported by four corner poles, wherein, Hugh knew, the congregation left the horses if the day proved inclement. Greenwood tugged at a rein. The mule left the pike and rounded the church. The cart came to rest beneath the roof shelter. The old man got down. Hugh, wondering and wary, got down too.

There was nothing to be wary about, not at the moment, for the old man now had something else on his mind.

During the exhibit at the stage house one of the figures, the most elaborate and expensive, Nebuchadnezzer and his chariot, had got out of order. Nebuchadnezzer, raising his sword aloft to strike, just froze in that futile position. Now Greenwood laid the figure on the cart-bed, got out

67

a few tools, and began to repair it.

The old man was incredibly deft and mechanical. Out came screws, wheels, springs, and cogs to be studied, oiled, adjusted. The concentration which emanated from him under the little shelter was as heavy as the drizzle outside.

It was then that the ungovernable seizure came over Hugh to leave this horrible man, this minute, now.

He turned toward the rear of the shelter and began to walk. Not to run, just to walk. The very fact that he was moving his leg muscles, doing something, going away, did a funny thing to him. He felt renewed, as he used to feel in the old days before this long nightmare had begun.

He had gone perhaps fifty feet in the drizzle when Greenwood noticed his absence and saw him and screamed, "Git back here!"

Now from behind Hugh came a torrent of abusive, savage cursing with a frantic overtone. Hugh turned his head.

The old man was coming after him and almost on him, stumbling, threshing, flailing his arms.

The quick view that he got of that contorted, malignant face, lips, soundless now and twisted, told Hugh that here was something else again. Greenwood was not dominated by the urge to get him back as a bondboy, by the

68

desire to recapture him for further servitude. He was being dominated by the lust of hate, by a desire to inflict punishment. Hugh did not allow himself to think what punishment might mean to this man.

He broke into a run, a dead run. Soon there was nothing behind him but the molten gray curtain of rain; nevertheless he continued to race. He fought his way through a dense salient of scrub, crossed, panting, a seemingly endless ankle-deep bog, and came out to dry land. Here, exhausted, he threw himself, weak and breathless, across the gnarled, knobby roots of an enormous tree. He closed his eyes.

A voice said to him sympathetically, "You in trouble, young feller?"

Hugh half-opened his eyes. Before him stood a square-jawed, stubble-faced man in clay-smeared work clothes. He carried a log chain in a big horny hand. Beside him was a workhorse; the horse had a homemade straw collar, the mark of utter poverty.

"I *was* in trouble," Hugh said. "But I think I left it behind me."

The man gave him a slow, solicitous smile. "That's what we always think," he said, "but somehow it doesn't generally work out that way. How would you like a little hot food?"

Food, and hot, thought Hugh. His canvas pouch was still across his shoulder, but, living high with Gadsby, he had forgotten to replenish it.

They exchanged names. The man's name was Martin St. Clair.

"I've been snaking logs all day," he said. Man, boy, and horse, they walked through the thin woods. "We don't have far to go. And Tib will have it waiting for us, hot."

V

He must have slept, Hugh realized now, when he had fallen to the ground after his big run, for it was night when they reached the timberman's cabin. Black, woolly, rainy night.

One window showed as they approached, a window with greased paper instead of glass. A yellow light was behind it. The small cabin was at the edge of a sizable forest pond, and the golden illumination struck across the gleaming blackness of the water to a dead, bonelike tree which had fallen in the pond's center. It was this tree that touched Hugh's heart. As a youngster he had seen many dead trees in a pond. In the summer there would be a kingfisher on this one, or a few turtles sunning themselves at its base. In the water there would be tadpoles, green scum, and small sunfish; and in the grass around the water's edge, frog-hunting copperheads, maybe. He went with St. Clair to a shed to stable the horse. This done, they opened the cabin's heavy slab door and stepped inside.

The small single room was frugal but exceptionally neat. The shredded tanbark on the floor was clean and new, and gave off a pleasant spicy smell. The barked logs had been whitewashed. There were two small beds, each in a corner of the room. Each bed was joined on its inner side by pegs into the wall. On its outer side each was supported by stakes driven into the earth floor. A girl of about nine years old, dressed in doeskin, gunny sacking, and calico—half Indian and half nothing—stood at the fireplace stirring a pot of thick gruel, made up, apparently, of coarse-ground yellow corn. She had limpid, dark-blue eyes. The callouses on her hands were nearly as heavy as those on her father's.

"Tib," said St. Clair. "This is Hugh Perrine. He's running from something, so don't ask no personal question nor pry."

The girl seemed hardly to hear. "We all run from something or other," she said casually. "I run from dragonflies, so they won't sew up my eyelids."

Hugh and the man sat on stools at a small table. She served them, then joined them, sitting across from Hugh.

Hugh, following their lead, stirred lard into the gruel and salted it with salt from a dried gourd. These people were very poor indeed, he thought. The food was eaten from wooden bowls with wooden spoons. There was no tea, nor coffee, nor milk. Just well water from a tin cup which they passed around.

The meal was eaten in silence. They were so sensitive to his feelings, so careful not to alarm him, that it was almost as though he wasn't there.

When he had finished, he felt enormously good and, somehow, very powerful. Then, hardly an instant later, exhaustion and weariness hit him like a blow of a hammer, and the urge to sleep seized him. He almost sprawled from his stool.

The child and her father, one on each side of him, took him gently by the arms and stood him up. They led him to the fireplace. The father took off Hugh's jacket. They laid Hugh on the floor before the hearthstone. The child laid his jacket across his legs. "It gets cold come daybreak," she said softly.

That was the last he remembered until he awoke in the morning.

There was no one in the room. His breakfast was on the table: more gruel, but this time a soft-boiled egg had been broken into it. A crisp slice of bacon had also been added. He suspected then and was sure later, when he remembered, that they had absented themselves while he ate because they could not afford to join him in such extravagance.

He ate gravely and went outside.

The child and her father were standing by the doorstep. In the east, a raspberry sun tinted a clear luminous sky.

"Nice day ahead," said Hugh.

St. Clair nodded. The child said, "Yes, nice."

He looked at them and they returned his gaze, smiling. He knew better than to try to pay them, than to offer these proud people money.

Moist-eyed, the child said, "Good luck."

"Tib!" her father said, "Jest say, come agin."

"Come agin," said the child.

Hugh, too moved to speak, to thank them, even to say good-by, raised his hand in farewell and left.

Before long he came to a narrow road which was scarcely a wagon's breadth wide. It was still thinly muddy from last night's drizzle. The lonesome looking back-road was hedged on either side by broken clumps of spiky thorn. To his right, almost directly over the road's center, rose the sun. That meant it ran east and west, generally, parallel to the main pike. Suddenly he decided this could be just the thing he needed. It went in the right direction for him. Greenwood would be searching for him on the pike. Feeling a little safer, he turned down it toward the sun.

The sun was nearly overhead when the little road took a dog-leg twist, and Hugh came abruptly upon the strange-looking building.

It was two stories high, boxlike, rickety, made of odds and ends of scrap lumber. Down the length of its side in three-foot letters was printed: "Emporium, Blacksmith, Stump Powder, Ladies Hats, Livery Stable." Across its front face, an outside stairway angled up to a second-story landing and an unpainted pine door, marked, "Reasonable Lodging." A big muscle-bound boy of about seventeen lolled on the bottom step of the stairway. His bullethead was cropped, he was dressed in shoddy mustard-colored wool, and his mean face was piggish. He was whittling a handle from a piece of cedar for a rusty old hunting-knife blade on his knee. He would cut a little, fit the two handle pieces over the knife's tang, then cut a little more.

When he saw Hugh, he said, "Who do you think *you*

are, and where do you think you're going?"

Hugh, ignoring him, walked past him and entered the ground-floor door beneath the staircase.

The shop inside was dim, pleasant smelling, and crammed with a jumble of wonderful things. There was about everything you could think of: spices, pig iron, china, hardware, tar, candy—everything. He stood at the counter and a waspish little woman with crescent-lensed spectacles swept up to face him and said, "What?"

"Five cents worth of dried peaches," said Hugh, "and five cents worth of crackers."

She got them together and laid them, loose, on the counter. He paid her and stowed them in his canvas pouch.

She wouldn't relinquish him. She said, "How about a little essence of almonds? It makes a good cake flavor."

"I believe not," said Hugh, "but thank you."

"A touch of it's nice on your hanky, or you can put it on your underwear, if you keer to go that far."

"No, ma'm."

"We got a specialty this week on milk-of-roses soap if you buy a dozen bars?"

"I think not," said Hugh.

"Was you quarrellin' with my baby boy out there, when you come in?"

"I don't quarrel with anybody," said Hugh, "if I can help it."

"Well, don't," said the woman. "He can tear you limb from limb if the mood strikes him. Just give him some of yore crackers and dried peaches if his elements starts to rise. That might mollify him."

"Thank you for the kind advice," said Hugh politely, and he went outside.

The big boy was standing just beyond the threshold. He stepped out, blocking Hugh's way as Hugh came forward.

"When I speak to you this time, I want you to answer me," he said threateningly. "Who do you think you are?"

This was a hard moment for Hugh. If there was one thing he had never been able to stand, it was for someone to try to bear down on him this way. But he had bigger troubles than this loudmouth. He had Greenwood.

"I'd like to tell you my name," said Hugh calmly. "But as you probably know, they got that law against it."

The big boy looked stupefied. "What law? What are you talkin' about?"

"The law that prevents a professional pugilist in transit from bragging about himself. If we was to go from place to place, throwing our weight around, somebody would always be challenging us for the glory of it, and we'd be leaving a swath of maimed behind us. And the law can't tolerate that."

The boy's eyes popped open and his jaw dropped. "You a prize fighter?"

"I didn't say that," said Hugh. "Remember, I didn't say that. But I'll tell you this. When I fight, if I do fight, but I don't say I do, I fight under the name of, 'The Genuwine Article.' "

"Whoosh!" said the boy, expelling his breath. "I never thought I'd be talking to a prize fighter. Will you shake my hand?"

"There's a law against that too," said Hugh. "But I'll do something even better. I'll take off my jacket and work out with you for five or six rounds."

"Gosh," said the boy, backstepping hastily. "I swear and declare I'd surely love to. But when I was a young un, I fell out of a apple tree and cracked my ribs. My ma wouldn't let me take the risk."

Hugh looked disappointed. "It wouldn't take long," he said. "A round, like you know, is a knock down. And I should be able to knock you down five times in five minutes, easy."

"That sounds like fun, all right," said the big boy. "But I got some wood to cut and better get to it. Good-by."

78

He vanished around the corner of the building. Hugh continued down the road.

He wondered what the road was doing to him. He'd handled it just as Joe Caffery would have handled it— with a quick tongue.

He ate the crackers and peaches, carefully saving some for his supper, about a mile farther on in a grassy little pocket enclosed by purple ironweed and lush goldenrod— and shared his meal with a dog. A big black dog with a rubbery underjaw and eyes that tried to speak shoved its coal-scuttle head through the weeds, stared at him, and came forward, wagging its tail almost as though this were a joyous reunion.

The dog ate three crackers and one dried peach. Actually, he didn't eat the peach. He was crazy about it, but he somehow couldn't bring himself to swallow it. It seemed to give him an appetite for the crackers though. He would chew on the peach for a while, making earnest faces, spit the peach out, and come over and ask for a cracker. He did this three times.

After they had eaten, Hugh picked a dozen fleas and four ticks off of the dog, took a bur out of the matted hair in his ear, and they went to sleep, Hugh on his back, the dog on his side with his spine pressed hard against Hugh.

When Hugh awoke and returned to the road the dog followed him, lumbering along beside him. The dog accompanied him for some distance, then sat down in the middle of the road and said as plainly as he could with his eyes, "This is as far as I go."

The friendly feeling that had come with the dog stayed on and got Hugh to thinking about Dan Nichols. They had something in common. They had each showed him an instant friendship which he sensed was honest and which he felt he could trust completely. Each had come and gone quickly and left him strangely lonely.

It wasn't logical, wasn't reasonable, but he missed Dan Nichols, missed him as he would an older brother who had been taken from him.

He thought of that moment of kindness Dan Nichols had displayed at Gadsby's campfire. He would always remember Joe Caffery as a brave and unselfish friend. But he would always remember Dan Nichols as a valiant protector.

Toward the middle of the afternoon the road widened a bit; a few more farmhouses appeared, and the countryside on left and right of him seemed somewhat better groomed and a little more prosperous. Milk cows increased, there were a few good bred sheep, and barns and houses were better roofed. Walking made Hugh thirsty.

He saw a house fifty yards or so from the road and turned down its lane.

It was a tall thin house with a front porch scarcely bigger than a wagon gate and having a little shelflike roof over it. A decrepit old man, maybe eighty, maybe a million, was asleep in a hickory rocker on the front porch. His mottled chin was atilt on his shoulder and his mouth was wide open. Hugh, observing the manners he had been taught as a youngster, stopped a short distance away and called, "Hello, the house!"

The old man awoke with a jerk, saw Hugh, and grinned. Hugh said, "Could I have a drink of water?"

The old man came nimbly off the porch, stood beside Hugh, peered at him, and said, "Sure. Gladly. Come along."

As they rounded the house to its rear the old man said, "I'm alone. The folks has gone off to celebrate a funeral. I got to stay and baste the roast. Where you from? Where you headed?"

"I'm bound for Cincinnati," Hugh said.

Behind the house, a few yards up a knoll, a small neat springhouse was set into the hillside. Hugh followed his host through the door and down three steps into the cellarlike rock-walled and rock-floored cubbyhole containing brown crocks of milk and food. The old man took

81

down a dipper, filled it from a springfed tank, and handed it to his visitor. "I made a trip to Cincinnati, once," he said. "Twenty-odd years ago. With a load of green hides. You ever smelt a load of green hides?"

"Yes," said Hugh.

"Well, a single load of hides is bad enough," said the old man. "But you ought to smell the warehouse where they stores them with their kith and kin. It's a scar to your mind and body that you never get over."

Hugh, with the dipper to his mouth, smiled.

He was standing so that the open door, about chest high, was slightly to his left. As he drank, his gaze went out the door. He could see down the slope to the left of the house and to the light-tan road in the near distance. He almost choked.

Greenwood's cart appeared on the road beyond the corner of the house from the west, moving east. Madly racing.

It was a terrible thing to look at. The clumsy old mule, goaded into a frenzy of speed, was throwing its hooves around wildly, like clods of dirt. Greenwood, leaning forward in the seat, seemed hardly to touch the seat itself, seemed to be crouching and hardly able to keep himself in leash. The cart, its wheels rattling and jolting, rolled on like an ineffectual cyclone.

82

Hugh watched with the dipper resting against his chest. He watched mule, man, cart pass. Watched them diminish. Watched them finally disappear.

The old man said, "What's wrong? Is they a bug in your water? If they is just take her out. Bugs won't hurt nobody. Unless it's a spider. From the way you're acting, I bet it's a spider."

"The water's fine," said Hugh, and he drank down the dipperful. "Thank you. I'd better be getting on."

"Would you like a little bait of food before you go?"

"I'd like it," said Hugh graciously. "But I haven't got the time."

When he left the old man he continued as he had been going but only until he had something between himself and the house, a cornfield. At the far edge of the cornfield he turned from the backroad to his right, directly into the countryside.

He was pretty sure that Greenwood had picked up his trail at the emporium—where the big boy had wanted to fight and then suddenly had wanted not to.

The worst thing now was that he knew Greenwood was a skillful tracker and was pursuing him as a man might play a game of chess—moves ahead. Greenwood was fighting Hugh with his mind, trying to read his brain.

Hugh had one advantage. Greenwood didn't know he had been seen.

The thing to do, Hugh decided, was to go back to his old route: the main pike south.

He began a slanting crosscountry walk, south by east. Crosscountry walking could be really rugged. He passed through grassy swales, climbed low-ridge spines, waded backcountry brooks. There was danger in this, too, because isolated farm women took a mighty bad fright sometimes at seeing a stranger climb a fence or a stile of theirs, and the men didn't relish it either. Trouble could start this way, serious trouble and quick.

Shortly before sunset when he felt he must be nearing his destination, the big pike, his direction was blocked by a seemingly endless belt of sassafras along a creek. He wondered whether to waste time going around its end or to thresh his way through it.

He fought his way directly into it, and it gave him quite a tussle.

VI

Hugh came out of the sassafras into a pasture scattered with stony outcrop. The pasture sloped gently upward to the rear of a barn. A short distance away and past the barn he saw the rear of a house. The barn was big and opulent looking, and the house beyond was more of a mansion than a house.

It was big and square and of white painted brick. On its roof stood four chimneys. The partial view he got of it beyond the barn eave showed it had a double back veranda, a deep porch below, and an upper porch with a fancy cast-iron railing. The upper porch was supported by six giant white pillars.

For the past hour Hugh had been unbearably thirsty. He decided to stop at the kitchen door and ask for a drink of water. Anybody would give anybody a drink of water.

Hugh was just passing the corner of the barn when he heard someone crying. It wasn't exactly crying. It was sort of a low spasmodic sobbing. He turned to his right and entered the open barn door. Inside, from the splintered timbered floor to the top of the hay mow, the barn seemed to be almost big enough to stable an average cabin.

The crying was coming from an open stall door, and he went to it to investigate. He saw a girl and a young colt. The colt was down with its legs out straight, and the girl was on her knees beside it. She had a handkerchief to her mouth and took it down when she saw him. She was about his age with soft brown hair and soft brown eyes, dressed in chalky daffodil-yellow linen, and about the loveliest thing he had ever run into.

He gave her a quick glance. Then because it was born in him to be solicitous about animals, he said, "What's wrong with him?"

"He won't eat. He won't touch food. He's starving. He won't go near his mother. I've heard colts were some-times that way."

"Well I never did," said Hugh. "Let me look at him."

The colt suddenly got up with a spring. He struck his belly with a hind foot, stamped a few times with a forefoot, and down he was on the stall floor again.

"He does that all the time," said the girl.

"You got a medicine chest in the house?" Hugh asked.

"Yes."

"Go in and bring me three ounces of spirits of turpentine, and an ounce of laudanum mixed in a half-pint of warm water in a good-sized bottle. Oh, yes. And a fresh egg."

She was off like a rocket.

Almost instantly, it seemed, she was back.

Hugh took the bottle from her hand. "Hold the egg," he said. "I'll ask you for it in a minute." He felt the glass of the bottle to see if he was satisfied with the temperature. He was.

"This colt has got colic," he said. He put the bottle far into the colt's mouth, gently, and poured the mixture down its throat.

"Now," he said. "We'll wait. We'll know in an hour whether to repeat the dose, adding powdered aloes, or whether this does it. There are lots of remedies for colic, but this is the one they say hardly ever misses. I've even seen children take it."

87

"Children!"

"Not so strong, of course. And with tea."

They stood and waited, sometimes studying the colt, sometimes each other.

Finally the colt staggered to its feet. It looked weak and bleary, but the wildness had left it.

Hugh grinned. The girl, relieved, started to weep once more, then stopped. "Now the egg," said Hugh.

He took the egg from the girl's hand. With one of his arms around the colt's neck to steady it, he tilted the head back, then put the egg in its mouth and broke it. "Now he's had a little meal," said Hugh, "whether he wanted to or not. I don't believe I've ever seen it done with colts, but it's an old trick with heifers."

The girl nodded, almost afraid to speak.

Hugh suddenly felt self-conscious.

"What I had in mind when I stopped in," he said, "was a drink of water."

"How about a glass of buttermilk instead?"

"That would be fine, but I don't want to put you to any trouble. Now if the colt doesn't nurse right away, baby him along with warm milk with maybe a little yeast in it."

"You can have the buttermilk now," she said. "And then in a little while we'll have supper."

88

"Oh, I can't stay for supper," he said, alarmed, thinking of his dusty clothes. "I have to move on. I'm on my way to Cincinnati."

"You don't travel at night, do you?"

"Of course not."

"Then, after supper you can spend the night."

Now he was truly terrified. But he could tell by the quiet smile at the corners of her lips that he was going to end up doing it and that nothing could change her.

Treating him like royalty, she took him into the house, not through the kitchen but around the side and in through the front door. As they passed the front he saw that it had a double veranda, too, like the back but much more elegant.

"I'm Cynthia Jeffers," she said. "What with one thing and another it slipped my mind to tell you."

"I'm Hugh Perrine," he said.

In the front hall a great staircase swept up to the third floor, its newel post and balustrade carved with vines and leaves. There was furniture here in the hall, a fact which surprised Hugh. There were tables and chairs and potted plants. Along one wall was a tall mahogany grandfather clock. Its dial said a quarter to seven.

"That clock can't be right," said Hugh. "It's not dark yet."

"It's broken, not even running," said the girl, "which is too bad. My father depends on it."

He followed her out of the hall, to the left, into a library. On all sides, bookcases filled with worn leather bindings rose to the ceiling. Where you could see a patch of wall, which was seldom, it was bright, deep blue. There were three or four ebony chairs with comfortable-looking cushions and, near them, several small knee-high tables. In the middle of the room there was a big table, ebony also, supported by a pedestal ending in three lion's paws, each paw holding a big glass ball. Each foot had bronze claws set into the wood and brightly polished. "Sit down," said Cynthia. "I'll be right back."

Hugh was sitting, resting his weary bones, realizing what exquisite pleasure there could be in just sitting when she returned.

A man came along with her. Hugh liked him on sight. He was short and solid. He wore drab worsted, and his waistcoat was mussy with cigar ashes.

Handing Hugh the buttermilk, Cynthia said, "This is my father. He wants to thank you about the colt."

"And about the girl too," said Mr. Jeffers. "She's been pretty miserable." He shoved out his hand. Hugh took it; it was calloused.

Mr. Jeffers sat down and beamed.

Hugh said, "I'd like to compliment you on your house. It's very fine." That was the opinion he felt it would be polite to express; his true opinion was one of confusion. He kept that to himself.

Mr. Jeffers said, "Mrs. Jeffers planned it. I think Cynthia and I might have come up with something, well, a little more domestic. However, we treasure it as a memory."

"My mother died three years ago," said Cynthia. "Typhoid."

Typhoid. The very same thing. Hugh said woodenly, "I was orphaned by typhoid myself. Both of them at once."

There was an interval of thick silence.

When the silence prolonged itself almost excruciatingly Mr. Jeffers said gravely, "Hugh, I've got a question to ask you. It is a little personal."

Now it comes, thought Hugh. I'm in his house, and he wants to know just what he's got on his hands. He's got a daughter to protect, and he has to know all about me. This is right and proper, of course. But what shall I tell him? The truth, all of it.

But the question, when it came, was asked with a smile. How would Hugh like his supper chop, rare or well done?

Before supper, Mr. Jeffers spoke of his life before he

had become a farmer. He had been a steamboat captain, had, in fact, later owned a line, but had retired to be with his daughter when her mother had died. He talked quietly, relaxing them, all through supper. They were served by a smiling, motherly housekeeper, who ate with them.

Once Mr. Jeffers said, "You know, Hugh, Cynthia's been on a fast herself. Know what I'm going to do next time she gets in that mood? Take my cue from you and break an egg in her mouth."

When the meal was over they returned to the library. Now, impulsively, Hugh told them all about himself. About his farming. About Joe Caffery, Gadsby, and Greenwood.

When Hugh had finished Mr. Jeffers said, "So you went into indenture for a friend. I had a feeling you were that kind of boy when I met you."

"So did I," said Cynthia.

After a moment's meditation Mr. Jeffers said, "Did it ever occur to you that this Greenwood might outguess you again?"

"What do you mean?" asked Hugh.

"You left the pike and went to the backroads. He did the same. Now you're back on the pike. It's like chess. Couldn't he come back too?" He paused. "The thing for you to do is hole-up here for a couple of days. If he comes back to the pike, let him get ahead of you. You're all right as long as he's ahead of you."

"At least a couple of days," said the girl.

"If he shows at taverns and taprooms," said Mr. Jeffers, "then it's not likely he'll be prowling around off-the-road residences like this one."

Hugh was overcome by such kindness "Thank you. I'd like to," he said.

"When does the colt get that warm milk and yeast?" asked Cynthia.

"This would be a good time, right about now," said Hugh. "I was just getting ready to excuse myself and do it."

"Cynthia will do it," said Mr. Jeffers. "I think I'd better put my travel-weary guest to bed."

Hugh's bedroom was about halfway down the broad second-story hall. Mr. Jeffers opened the door, gave him a little pat on the shoulder, and waved him in to his privacy. He tried not to embarrass Hugh with too much formality.

Inside, Hugh shut the door and turned to look things over. The room was small and very pleasant, but something that Hugh had never even imagined. The house-keeper had already come and gone, folding down the bed clothes, lighting the ruby-glass whale-oil lamp on a small nightstand by the bed's head. The bed itself was something to look at twice. It was a tall poster. The tops of the posts had been carved into pineapples. The smoky lampwick made a little prison of feeble golden light, scarcely extending to the dark moss-green walls. A high birch chest of drawers in a corner threw off buttery highlights. Hugh undressed to his drawers, put his clothes and pouch on a chair seat and his shoes neatly beside the chair legs, put out the lamp, and crawled into bed. The sheets, fresh from a linen closet, had a clean sweet scent of lavender sachet. Instantly, he was sound asleep.

The next morning he descended the front stairs to the hall. He had hardly reached the bottom step by the newel post when Mr. Jeffers came out of the library to meet him. "The colt's fine," said Mr. Jeffers. "Or will be soon. How did you rest?"

"On that feather bed?" said Hugh. "Wonderful. But I'm afraid I got that face towel dirty. Forget-me-nots and all."

"That's what it's for," said Mr. Jeffers.

At midmorning Hugh was sitting alone on a white painted iron bench on the front veranda, with dead leaves around his ankles, when Cynthia came around the corner of the house. Under her arm, she had a small hamper of split cane. She said, "Let's take a little walk."

Hugh left the porch and joined her.

He went with her as she retraced her steps back around the building. They passed the relic of a kitchen garden, passed a cluster of sheds, and came to an indistinct foot path. Following the path, they climbed a rise, descended, and made their way through a swale of sere, yellow swamp grass. By noon the path had long since vanished. Finally she said, "Here we are. This is the place."

There was a stream here, reduced to a tiny ribbonlike trickle because of the dry weather. On one side of the stream, their side, was a low bank, like a beach. It was studded with polished pebbles and little knots of turf, many of them still green. Across the stream the bank was high, about six feet, and undercut by past floods, with clay arches reaching up and under and out from stream level to the fringe of grass above. A great elm grew on top of this bank across from them, and its roots hung down, exposed, in a beautiful and intricate filagree.

She opened the hamper and laid out food. They sat cross-legged and ate.

"I come here all year," she said, "even when it's winter."

He gave her a hard look. Chewing a bite of sandwich, he asked, "Why?"

"There's a little vein of salt by the stream over there

beneath those roots. Animals come here."

"Animals?"

"Wild ones."

She told him about it happily. "Deer mainly," she said. "If you're careful, they'll come. Once there was a mother bear and her cub. They became frightened and disappeared just before I got here. I just missed them."

"Missed them? Then how do you know they were here?"

"I saw their fresh tracks."

He looked skeptical. "You can tell tracks? And not only tracks, but fresh tracks?"

"Oh, sure," she said. "That's one of the main reasons I like to come, the tracks. The night animals I never see at all—just their tracks. Bobcat and possum and raccoon, for instance."

"Do you know something?" he said. "I think a raccoon is the prettiest animal God ever created."

"I favor a fox," she said.

He looked startled. He had never heard anyone say a good word for a fox before.

"They don't run," she said. "They flow. They're beautiful."

Before they realized it the sun was low in the western sky, cherry red, filmed with October haze, and it was time for them to go.

As they came into the houseyard, they stopped by the barn. The colt looked fine to Hugh. "Unless I miss my guess," he said, "he'll be nursing very soon."

They started around the house to the front door. Hugh said, "You know something? What with one thing and another, I never did get around to asking you the colt's name?"

"Maple Sugar. He's that soft creamy tan."

Hugh winced. "A boy colt? I mean does it seem just right? How about Thunderbolt? Or——"

"He likes it the way it is."

"Look at it this way," said Hugh earnestly. "Say he's grown and out in a pasture, and you call him. You shorten his name, naturally, and call out, Maple! People are going to think you're saying Mabel."

"Then I'll shorten it to Sugar," she said comfortably.

They both laughed.

They went up the front steps, across the porch, and into the hall, laughing. Almost immediately Cynthia said, "Look. Someone has fixed the clock."

Hugh glanced at the tall grandfather clock. It was throwing out crisp-sounding clicks, and its pendelum was swinging gracefully.

Now Mr. Jeffers was standing by their side, very seri-

97

ous. "Yes," he said. "This afternoon a clock-mender dropped by. He fixed it very cheaply, by the way. He seemed most to want to talk. He wanted to know if I'd seen a strong, big-chested boy of about fifteen, who wore a canvas pouch on a leather thong across his shoulder. This was an oldish kind of man with dirty gray hair hanging down from his hat, sort of across his face."

"Greenwood," said Hugh.

This made sense. If Greenwood could repair his mechanical figures with such dexterity, it was very likely he could mend clocks as well.

Hugh said, "Just a minute." He pushed past them, went upstairs, and returned with his pouch. "Good-by," he said. "I must go."

They were shocked.

"No," said Cynthia.

"He's come and gone," said Mr. Jeffers. "There's nothing really to be alarmed about."

"I'm not afraid for myself," said Hugh. "I'm afraid for you. You don't know that man."

He had threatened to burn Gadsby's wagon, and everyone who had heard him speak had known he had meant it.

If he hadn't moved on but was still loitering in the vicinity and had learned, somehow, that Hugh was here, he wouldn't hesitate, some dark night, to fire the Jeffers' home.

"You've been good friends to me," Hugh said.

Then, before they could break his will, before they could convince him to remain against his better judgment, he departed.

Outside, as he walked down the front drive he didn't turn around. They didn't call but he knew they were in the doorway, watching him.

VII

As Hugh left the mouth of the Jeffers' driveway, he saw that he had calculated the direction correctly, and he found himself again on the big pike. He hitched the thong of his pouch over his shoulder to seat it comfortably and once more headed east toward faraway Cincinnati.

The thing to do, he thought, was to follow Mr. Jeffers' advice and to keep Greenwood ahead of him—if he could. But how could you tell if you were behind or ahead of him, the cunning way he had of outguessing your mind?

The thing to do was to cut around all villages and towns, to skirt them at the rear. Greenwood could very well be lingering in any of them. However, Hugh decided,

he would have to take a chance on the first one. He was
faced with the same old traveling problem: he had to lay
in a supply of road food again.

At a small crossroads store, a store which, actually, was
the front room of a farmer's cottage, he bought eggs and
cornmeal and was given a piece of bacon rind. There was
no sign of Greenwood. This raised his spirits.

When the store was behind him he left the pike, cutting back into undergrowth, looking for a place to cook
and eat his supper, a safe place, with water if he could
find any.

He was in no real hurry. After a bit, he found himself
in wild desolate terrain. A stream, flattish and serpentine,
meandered through a forest of looming beeches. The air
was utterly still, without a whisper of breeze, and October
night fell, crystal blue, as he built his fire at the brook's
edge. Lonesome for the Jefferses, he prepared his meal.

From his pouch, he took a skillet, a small pan, and a
tin plate. In the skillet he cooked the bacon rind until
it was crisp. Then he removed it and put it, for the time
being, in his plate. Now he fried three eggs in the bacon
grease in the skillet. While the eggs were frying, he put
cornmeal and water into the pan and stirred it to a thick
paste. Now he took the bacon rind from his plate, where
it had cooled a little and he could handle it, crumbled it,

and added it to the cornmeal. He removed the cooked eggs from the skillet, put them into the plate, and, having molded the cornmeal into pones, cooked the pones in the skillet. He washed his pan while the pones cooked, half-filled the pan with water, and, nudging the skillet over a little, boiled his nine remaining eggs. These with the left-over pones would be his traveling food. The pones cooked, he ate some with the fried eggs; they were as good as crackling-bread.

When he finished his supper, he started back to the pike in a wide half-circle. It was his idea to sleep close to the road, but not too close, someplace where he could look it over carefully before he resumed his journey.

He had gone some distance when a small black structure with a glow of yellow firelight among the beech boles loomed up in his path. As he approached, he saw what he had always heard called a half-faced cabin. It was scarcely as tall as a man, and its roof, high at the back, sloped from back to front. Its front was open. Roof and sides were covered with stiff deer hides. The front, too, could be covered with hides, but these were now drawn, leaving an open view of the inside.

It was the sort of structure, makeshift and easy to erect, once favored by hunters but now favored by outcasts and idlers too lazy to put up a more substantial shelter.

A fire was on the earth before it, illuminating the interior.

A half-faced cabin always had a big base-log at its back. This had one too, and on the ground in front of it was a bearskin pallet. A man lay sprawled on the pallet, holding and chomping a roasted saddle of rabbit. When he looked up and saw Hugh passing, he yelled, "Hey! Hold on there!"

Hugh came to a stop. The man got up and came out.

"What?" Hugh asked.

"Nothin'," said the man. "Anybody come into my front yard, I want to take a look at 'm."

He was about thirty and garbed in an old-time greasy knee-length hunting shirt. It was out of style in this part of the country, and Hugh was convinced he wore it to make people stare at it and point at him. He had tiny predatory eyes set way back behind a long sharp weasel nose. A thin red beard was almost like red fuzz on his chin.

"Set and visit a while," he said.

"I've got to be getting on," said Hugh.

"When I say set, set!" said the man with the beginning of a snarl.

After a moment's consideration, Hugh dropped to his haunches. The man sat on his heels across the fire from him.

Hugh couldn't think of anything to say. He didn't need to, because what the man really wanted was someone to talk at.

He talked about a festered tooth he had just gotten over, how to make a fiddle string, the best way to skin a catfish. He talked about the wealthy farmers roundabout with ill-concealed cupidity; and the feeling grew on Hugh more and more that the man was a sneak thief and petty pilferer.

He got talking about how to cheat in a horse trade, and then about horses generally, and then he said, "Talking about horses, I seen three beauties the other day."

A chill went down Hugh's spine. "Three?" he said. "All at once? Where?"

"At a town back down the pike. They was a feller putting on a show, riding them up and down Main Street. I have to admit he was a pretty good horseman. Nigh as good as I am. I might shade him a little, but not much. You should have saw it."

"I wish I had," said Hugh quietly.

"You headin' east or west?"

"East."

"Then if you hustle you might catch him at Archersburg, about four mile east of here. I hear tell he's due to put on the same show there tomorrow forenoon."

Hugh lapsed into silent reverie. Dan Nichols, he thought. What will he say? How will he look when he sees me again? Will he smile, or frown, or what? What if he doesn't even remember me? And when you came right down to it, why should he?

Suddenly, he was aware that the man across the fire from him, talking on and on, was making a disturbing statement.

He was saying, "Yes, sir. Times have changed. When I was a sprout, travelin', I was lucky to be carryin' a big copper penny on me. These days, young fellers like you, travelin' from place to place, think nothing of toting ten, twenty dollars on their person."

"Listen," said Hugh. "Talking about money, seems like I've run into nothing but bad luck. You appear to be a reasonable and human sort of man. Do you think if I hung around until morning you might have a little work for me to do for my breakfast?"

"No," said the man curtly.

"I've got a A-1 jackknife with only one broken blade," said Hugh, "that I'm going to sell cheap to some lucky fellow."

"Don't bother to take it out of your pocket," said the man with a sneer. He spat into the fire. "Well, you've took up enough of my time. Get up, and forward march."

Hugh got up, blank faced. Hesitantly he said, "When I first came up, you had a rabbit bone in your hand. Would you care to tell me where you throwed it?"

"I et it," said the man harshly. "Now move on."

Hugh moved on.

There I go again, he thought. Quick with the fancy lie, like Caffery. I really have become a roadboy.

That night, sleeping in a little ravine a stone's throw from the pike, he suffered severely from cold. As he ate his breakfast, he realized that this was going to become a graver and graver problem. Perhaps, if he asked politely enough, he could sleep in farmers' barns. Most farmers, though, were mighty touchy about strangers in their barns. He would be himself. A farmer's barn and its contents were his most important property.

Hugh had another problem too—even more critical. Last night in his excitement at the prospect of seeing Dan again, he had simply wished it away. This morning it faced him. And it was a stark one.

Should he go to Archersburg to see Dan and risk meeting Greenwood?

Actually, he didn't have to give it a second's thought. The answer was that he would risk meeting a hundred

Greenwoods for one Dan Nichols.

He had walked along the road about a mile and was passing through giant chestnuts—when he heard the loud clapping of breaking wood and the squeal of grinding metal coming from somewhere in front of him. He began to run in that direction.

The forest ended abruptly, and he came out into the open. On his left was a knoblike hill, covered with tiny cedar seedlings. The pike looped around the knob's base, and here, as he came up in a lope, he saw the accident.

A stage had upset while making the turn. Luckily, Hugh saw instantly, it had been empty except for the driver. These upsets, or capsizes as they were called in the trade, were not infrequent, and with the globe-shaped passenger compartment swinging so high above the axles that way, many a driver took what they called the lofty toss. When a capsize happened, say at full speed with a jammed-in load, the mayhem could be horrible.

Now the coach body lay on its side at the side of the road, one wheel spinning; the road itself was littered with a torn-off door and splintered spokes. It was a four-horse stage. One horse was down. The others, frantic eyed, stood in a tangle of harness. The driver was trying to calm the standing horses and get the fallen horse to its feet.

Hugh stepped forward and helped. He quieted the standing horses while the driver got the other erect.

For a moment neither Hugh nor the driver spoke, each tending to his own business.

Finally, when things were under control, the driver said, "Thanks."

He was a solid little man in rumpled clothes. Hugh looked at his face closely; it was coarse pored and slit eyed. He looked at it angrily, for he had always heard that some stage drivers were heavy drinkers. They claimed they had to be to stand the pace, because of the rough schedules and long hours they had to keep. In Hugh's opinion, any man who would do this to a team of horses because he was drunk ought to be taken out behind the barn and shot.

This man wasn't drunk, though, he soon realized. And, more than that, he was a mighty good man. For one thing, he had blood down the side of his face and wasn't paying any attention to it. For another, most drivers, certainly, would be worried about the big money loss because of the shattered coach, but this driver worried only about the frightened horses and how to sooth them.

"What happened?" asked Hugh.

"The bay here," said the driver, "is skittish. When I was making the turn she shied at a patch of milkweed down that blowed up against her face. She had a little fit and her friend caught it and they capsized us."

"Will they fire you?" asked Hugh.

"No, the bay has a kind of sorry reputation around the stables as being scarey. Poor beasts. They can't help the way they are. It's our duty to take care of them."

Hugh nodded in understanding agreement.

It was then that he noticed the man's boots, and he caught his breath. He had seen those identical boots before. They were Joe Caffery's cavalry boots. Caffery had worn his pants tucked into them. This man wore his pants legs over them; that was why Hugh hadn't noticed them immediately. But these were the same boots, all right. Patch on patch, rundown heels, and warped toes. He would never forget them. There weren't, there couldn't be, two pairs of boots like that in the whole wide world.

It came into Hugh's mind that Joe Caffery was dead, that he had died a homeless boy among strangers. They had peddled some of his effects to help pay for his burial in some friendless potter's field.

"Those boots," said Hugh tautly. "Where did you get them?"

"You like them?" said the driver. "They ain't much to look at, but I can tell you they're comfortable. I got them for only a shilling about fifteen miles down the pike off on a side road at a little town called Corlock."

"From who?" said Hugh. "Who sold them to you?"

"A puny, sickly looking young fellow in gray gingham. We never give each other our names. I just bought them and walked away."

Joe Caffery himself. So Caffery wasn't dead after all.

But in a way it was almost as bad. Joe, starving, was reduced to selling his clothes. Was he barefoot now with winter coming on? I'll have to look him up, Hugh decided grimly. Look him up and divide my money with him.

A stage coach packed with passengers came thundering around the knoll from the west. With a shriek of its brakes it pulled up and stopped alongside them. The new coach was from a rival line, and Hugh was to learn later that this was a great act of humanity on the new driver's part, for the policy between rival lines was cutthroat, dog-eat-dog.

The two drivers exchanged remarks, and the new driver said he would report the capsize at the next town, Archersburg, and have help sent out.

"Archersburg?" said Hugh. "I'm bound for Archersburg. What might the fare be?" He was desperate not to miss Dan Nichols, and he had already lost time here at the wreck.

"The fare is about three cents a mile," said the new

driver. "Archersburg is about two miles yet. I'll let you have it for a half-dime."

"I'll pay it," said the other driver. "It's the least I can do."

"Oh, no you won't," said Hugh. "And get that head cut fixed."

At a gesture from the new driver, he climbed up and sat on the box beside him. There was a cracking and snapping of the long whip and the coach was off, the wind whipping around Hugh's ears and everything wobbling and jolting and swaying. It was his first ride on a stage. He felt suspended high in the air. Now he knew what a capsize really meant.

They were in Archersburg, it seemed, almost before he had time to dig out his money and pay the man.

In size, Archersburg proved to be somewhere between a village and a very small town. A thin thread of people lined each side of Main Street, facing each other. Many, Hugh noticed, held Dan Nichols' yellow handbill in their hands. The stage rolled briskly between them, turned into a side street, and stopped at the stage office. Hugh dismounted and returned to the crowd. There had been no sign of Dan.

Hugh managed to get a place in the front between a couple of townsmen who talked to each other across him.

"You ever see this fellow before?" one asked the other.

"Ever' year for three years. I wouldn't miss him."

"Folks comes from all over this end of the county. It's good for trade."

Hugh thought of Piltonville, the hotspot, and how it hadn't allowed Dan to show.

The first man said, "And he does it with Morgans, and Morgans is trotters."

"But mighty brainy trotters. He trains 'em young special for this; he told me last year."

Clearing his throat, Hugh asked courteously, "When does it start?"

The man on his left looked at his watch. "In about twelve minutes."

Those twelve minutes seemed twelve hours.

VIII

THE CROWD STILLED. Dan came walking lazily down the
center of the street, dressed in moss-green trousers and a
white shirt. His shoes looked like soft buckskin moccasins,
but not quite like moccasins either. He was a thin man
but you could see that under the cloth, muscles lay on him
in flat bands and tight ropes. Behind him, like pets, unled,
came the beautiful, perfectly matched horses. Dan came
to a stop at the edge of the road, and the horses came to
a stop too, a little behind him, patiently, bridle reins
hanging over their necks.

Now, relaxed but loud and clear, Dan began to speak.
He said, "Those of you who have seen me before know

there will be no donations here, or collections. This is a demonstration and exhibition put on entirely and solely as a compliment and courtesy for the Blue Ash Stock-breeding Farm."

At this, there was a handclap or two.

Dan bowed deeply, grinning, and said, "Our first demonstration will be Tartar style."

He snapped his fingers and one of the horses detached itself from the others, trotted down the road, danced to a turn, and came forward in a thunderous volley of hooves.

Dan crouched, catlike. Just as the horse passed him, he caught it by the tail, and, somehow, in the same motion swung himself astraddle its back. Now came the turn again, and once more the horse came back, churning and wild eyed. All the while Dan Nichols was dismounting at its side, mounting, dismounting, mounting. Hugh, frozen, watched with his lips parted.

"Next," said Dan when the act was finished. "Plains Indian style."

Now he rode the second horse, pressing himself flat against one side like a leech. Up and back, up and back. If you were on yon side of him, the horse seemed riderless. Hugh could see that Dan was undergoing great physical strain here. Making this circuit but twice, he seemed knotted and flushed when it was over.

The third display, he called Roman style. Here he led his horses, all three of them, to the middle of the road, lined them up abreast carefully, and mounted. He mounted so that each of his feet was on an outside horse. The center horse was beneath him. He gathered the reins in his hand, and this time his rein hand was gloved.

He rode them between the double line of people, down full length of the crowd, and turned them.

Now he came—first at a walk, a short distance at a jog, then at a dead run.

The horses came down the center of the road in a tight knot. They passed Hugh like a cyclone, manes flying, eager, teeth bared, fetlocks threshing rhythmically, glossy necks arched in joy and excitement. Above them in a nimbus of golden dust, was a man, Dan, but somehow the man seemed nothing, the glorious animals everything.

Then it was all over, and Dan Nichols and his horses were gone. The crowd sighed.

One of the men standing next to Hugh spoke to him. "Right now, right this very minute, can you recite the alphabet?"

"No," said Hugh..

"I can't myself," said the man.

"If I wanted a word with him, I wonder where I might find him?" asked Hugh.

"When he's in town," said the man, "he generally stays yonder." He pointed to a sign about a block away.

The sign said, "President Polk." It hung out over the sidewalk on an iron bracket. The building itself was square and constructed of purplish brick. It was not too large, but from the way the stone doorstep and the stone window facings had been scrubbed to snowy white, Hugh felt in his bones that it was mighty expensive. He twisted the big brass doorknob and stepped inside.

He found himself in a small cubelike anteroom. He faced the blank brick wall of a five-foot-wide chimney base which stood a few yards in front of him. A staircase was tucked in a corner by the chimney. Hugh was a little shy and came to a halt. To his left, an open door showed a kitchen, its low rafters hung with herbs and onions and smoked meats. A woman worked briskly at a butcher's chopping block. At his right slatted doors, varnished bright yellow, swung wide. He could see a small section of the inn parlor, the mahogany paneled walls, an expensively dressed man seated at an expensive-looking table with a silver tankard of hot cider before him. He was sprinkling red pepper into it. Hugh's father had liked red pepper in hot cider.

A leathery-faced man came out of the parlor and confronted Hugh amiably. He had a military bearing, stood ramrod straight, and was dressed like a gentleman—in superfine broadcloth and with no apron. It took Hugh an instant or so to realize this man was the proprietor here.

"I'm Captain Anthony," he said good humoredly. "What can I do for you?"

Hugh asked about Dan Nichols.

"He is in his room," said the military gentleman. "I'll take you up to him." He didn't seem to think Hugh's travel-worn farm clothes at all unusual.

He led Hugh to the staircase and ascended. The stairs spiraled the chimney, and they came up into a landing on the second floor with doors opening on it. The chimney shaft continued its rise in the landing's center.

Captain Anthony knocked on one of these doors. When Dan Nichols' voice called out from within, he said, "You've got a guest," and left.

Dan opened the door. He was in smoking robe and carpet slippers, and was tamping tobacco from a twist of newspaper into his meerschaum pipe.

"I hoped I'd see you again," he said calmly. "You were in trouble that night, weren't you? I've worried about it ever since. Come in."

"Yes," said Hugh, entering. He was calm and un-frightened at the importance of the moment, because Dan himself was so calm and natural. "I was in trouble then, and I'm in worse trouble now."

"Maybe yes, maybe no," said Dan mildly. "Sit down and let's hear about it. But first——!"

He left the room, was gone about two minutes, and re-turned.

"Food," he said. "It'll be along shortly."

The walls, of tongue-and-groove pine, had been painted a restful, smoky green. There was a thick brown rug on the floor. There were also a low-slung bed of satinwood; three massive chairs, painted black and gold; a wash-stand; and a tall black wardrobe with a little painting of a ship in a storm on it. A small window with leaded bubble-glass panes opened on a view of the back court-yard and its immaculate stable. Hugh, suddenly shy again, seated himself in silence.

There was a knock at the door and a boy with a button nose and in cut-down clothes came in, carrying a light table and a willow-withe basket. He put down the table and set it with tableware from the basket. He looked everywhere but at Hugh, and Hugh was glad to see him leave.

Now the woman Hugh had seen in the kitchen entered

with an enormous silver salver which she put on the table. On the salver was sliced ham, broiled chicken, kidney beans, mashed turnips, sweet potatoes, jams, jelly, white bread, and butter. She gave the table a hard inspection and left.

She had hardly gone, when Captain Anthony marched in and made his inspection too. "It had better be perfect," he said, "or heads will roll in the kitchen."

"It'll be perfect," said Dan. "It always is."

When the Captain too had vanished, Hugh said, awed, "He sure respects you."

"I respect him too," said Dan. "He was with Jackson at New Orleans, and was left for dead in the swamp. Well, let's eat."

He served himself casually and ate. After some hesitation, Hugh followed suit.

It was a better meal, even, than he had had at the Jeffers. For one thing, here he wasn't with strangers. He was with an old friend. When they had finished, Dan placed the table and dishes outside the door, sank into an easy chair, and said, "Now let's talk about your trouble. Have you run away from that peddler? What was his name, Gadsby?"

Hugh said, "Gadsby lost me by default in a chicken match to a showman named Greenwood. I've run away

119

from Greenwood."

"Lost you?"

"Assignment of interest. He endorsed the indenture over to this Greenwood. But neither of them really had any hold on me, you see, because I'm not Joe Caffery. I'm Hugh Perrine."

Dan Nichols seemed unsurprised. "Listen," he said. "Why not tell me the whole story?"

Hugh did. He told it slowly from the beginning, bringing in every detail. First, he explained to Dan just who he was and about his going to Cincinnati to look for work.

Here Dan made his first comment. "What kind of work? Ax-farming?"

"Any kind of work," said Hugh. "I'm healthy."

He told about the Merry Fifer and how the innkeeper had tried to charge him two dollars for a basin of coffee and a piece of gingerbread—and how Joe Caffery had stood up for him.

Then, to emphasize Caffery's bravery and sacrifice, he explained how Caffery had so acted in spite of being a fugitive.

"This Joe Caffery," said Dan slowly, "sounds like a pretty fine sort of human. I'd like to hear a little more about him."

"I don't know too much about him," said Hugh. "We

didn't talk very long. He had to hit for the brush. Gadsby bound him from his uncle out in Illinois. Then the uncle spent the indenture money and died, so there was no way, no way at all, that Caffery could get out of it. He was doomed for life until he was twenty-one."

"Why did Caffery run away?" asked Dan. "Was Gadsby cruel to him?"

"At times, in streaks, Caffery said. But all in all not too bad. He just said there was no future in being an apprentice to a backwoods peddler."

"And he wanted to better himself."

"Wouldn't you?"

"Yes," said Dan. "I would."

Hugh then recounted how he had allowed himself to be taken as Caffery to allow Caffery more time to get away. And how Gadsby thought he had done this in destitution and was satisfied.

"And you did this to repay your friend," said Dan.

"No," said Hugh. "Not to repay him. I did it because he *was* my friend. You don't repay friends."

Then he related the incident about the cockfight that didn't come off and told Dan about Greenwood, his new master. As he spoke, his voice became so carefully unemotional that Dan said, "Greenwood is a different story isn't he? You're afraid of Greenwood."

121

"Yes," said Hugh. "He's horrible. He was going to break my will by starving me."

"But you knew that you didn't belong to him, that you didn't belong to anybody, that you weren't Joe Caffery, that you could have run away any time the notion struck you—which is exactly what you did. Forget him."

"Nobody could ever forget Greenwood," said Hugh. He described his looks and his strange, crazy cruelty. "He wouldn't care whether the paper was legal or not. He said he gave twenty dollars and two gamecocks for me and was going to keep me. He said if I ran away he'd dearly love to hunt me down, and he has been doing it too."

Dan Nichols studied the brown hairs on his wrist.

"It's a very ugly picture," he said wearily, "but thank goodness it's all over now. There's something else, Hugh, something I missed when I read that contract that night in the feeble firelight. You say Joe Caffery had been indentured in Illinois? Then he is free too, and has always been free since the moment Gadsby took him out of the state. A master cannot transport a bondboy for service over a state line. If so done, the contract is voided. And this is a fact Gadsby must have very well known. What manner of men are these who walk the roads and byroads these days? Gaining ascendency over youngsters by fraud, terror, and an occasional crust of bread?"

Hugh could hardly believe his ears.

"You say Caffery's free, too?" he asked, stunned.

"I've told you the law of the land, Hugh Perrine," said Dan, "and nothing can alter it."

Hugh then told him about the wrecked stage, the driver, and the boots. "Joe Caffery thinks right now he's a criminal," said Hugh. "We've got to get to this town Corlock so you can put him straight. Besides, if he's selling his clothes, he needs help."

"We'll find him," said Dan gravely, "and tell him. Immediately. And if he needs help, we'll give him all he can use. That's a promise."

Outside the window, autumn dusk was staining the sky. Hugh was under Dan's wing now. They both knew it, and were both happy about it. Dan got him quarters that night in the room next door, a room exactly like Dan's.

There were a long-handled brush and a sponge on the washstand. Hugh gave himself a good rough bath before he went to bed.

With the lamp out and clean sheets and a fluffy blanket up to his chin, he closed his eyes blissfully. It was almost beyond belief how the world could be so wretched and frightening one minute and so perfect the next.

IX

It was midmorning the next day when Dan came into Hugh's room and awakened him. He woke him by putting a tray of food, jellied veal, hot biscuits and honey, and coffee, under Hugh's nose. Hugh grinned, got out of bed, brushed his teeth vigorously at the wash stand, and got to work wordlessly, putting the biscuits and veal where they belonged. After he had eaten and dressed, they went down the spiral stairs, through the anteroom, and out on to the sidewalk. Dan's three beautiful horses were at the inn hitching-rack, groomed and ready to go.

And two, not one, had saddles.

"I'm not going to ride one of those beautiful animals,"

said Hugh doggedly. "They're show animals. Suppose I should hurt it some way? If we happen to be going the same direction, I say if we happen to, then I can walk beside you."

"We happen to be going in the same direction. You've ridden before, haven't you?"

"A little."

"Then mount, and let's be getting on to Corlock," said Dan. "That one there, her name's Athena. This one is Minerva. I ride Diana. They're Morgans as you've probably noticed. Morgans are not saddle horses, of course, but these have been especially trained. Do you know anything about Morgans?"

"Not much. Plow horses are more my style, or have been."

"Sometime back the breed wasn't too well known, but now it's becoming immensely popular. When the light vehicle came along Morgans were bred for it. For trotting and road speed. These particular horses are something a little different, of course. For public exhibition."

Hugh looked them over, trying to judge their points.

"They must have cost you real money," he said.

"What they cost me," said Dan, "was time and patience."

When Hugh had mounted, he said, "This saddle. Do

you always travel with an extra saddle?"

"No," said Dan. "I went out and bought it while you were asleep; it's secondhand but serviceable."

After a moment Hugh said, "Bought it for me? Just for me? Do you expect for me to be with you that long?"

"If you decide to leave," Dan said carelessly, "I can always sell it. Saddles are easily negotiable."

"You say we're headed for Corlock," said Hugh. "What about your dates, your show dates in between?"

"My show dates are elastic. I make them when the mood hits me, and don't if it doesn't. We'll talk that subject over again after Corlock."

They left the inn rack and started down the pike. Hugh's magnificent mount was like an elixir in his body.

"First we come to a place called Deevers Ford, about ten miles down the road," said Dan. "At Deevers Ford, we turn left on a side road. Corlock is a few miles down that side road. We should get there at about nine tonight."

It was suppertime and dark when their horses waded the shallow stream which crossed the road and gave Deevers Ford its name. The town began on the opposite bank: a scattering of cabins first, then houses and cabins which thickened to a brightly lamplit business center. Here, everything was abustle. "Market day," said Dan, and Hugh nodded in agreement; it was a familiar scene to him. He had never ridden ten miles on a horse before and his muscles ached.

Flares burned from stanchions along the sidewalk, and everywhere there were people, women and children, men and dogs—standing still, in movement, laughing, yelling, arguing. There were two or three sidewalk stalls, offering food for adults and doing a big suppertime trade. A solitary hawker pushed here and there, selling tidbits attractive to children: parched horse corn, salted, to be eaten like nut kernels; and small mouth-sized balls of molasses candy.

"Want to get down and stretch your legs?" asked Dan.

"I'm fine," said Hugh. "I'm just getting limbered up. I could go on all night."

"That barbecued shoat looks pretty good."

"Well if you put it that way," said Hugh.

They dismounted. Dan vanished into the crowd while Hugh held the horses. When Dan returned, he held a half-loaf of bread and a slab of six spareribs in each hand. They ate in silence, bread, meat, bread, meat, dropping the bones one by one on the ground. When they had finished, they licked their fingers and smiled. "Pretty good," said Dan. "Wonderful," said Hugh.

Dan examined the knot of Diana's lead rope at his

cantle, mounted, and picked up his reins.

Hugh had his hand on Athena's saddlehorn, his foot in the stirrup, and was about to swing himself up when he felt the tug on his sleeve.

The tug was so light it was almost feathery. He glanced down at the cuff of his sleeve. Grimy, skeletonlike fingers held a little nip of it, and, as he gazed, yanked once more. He turned.

It was Greenwood. His lips were lifted in a mirthless smile, showing yellow teeth that were filmed with a mossy scum. The pupils in his eyes looked like the sharp ends of tiny slivers of glass. He said, "To the gates of perdition."

When Hugh, turned to stone, didn't answer, Green-wood said in a velvet voice, "I've got a rusty piece of old hacksaw blade in the palm of my hand. Raise your voice and I'll jugulate you."

Hugh glanced desperately at Dan. Scarcely two feet away, Dan was sitting his saddle, watching, listening, doing nothing. In fact he seemed hardly interested.

"You've led me quite a chase," said Greenwood. "You know what I'm going to do?"

"What?" said Hugh.

"I'm going to take you to a cave I know of, south of here, down in the forest by the river. You know why?"

It seemed a dream to Hugh. Dan was just sitting there, doing nothing, looking even slightly entertained.

"No," said Hugh. "Why?"

"So I can take a pistol in one hand to protect myself and a whip in the other," said Greenwood, "and work on you until I make you a helpless old man just like me."

Now Dan was on the ground, standing by Hugh's side. When he spoke, it was to Hugh. He said, "I'm sorry. I didn't know it was going to be this bad, or I would have moved in sooner."

Greenwood, stepping back, said angrily, "Who is this?"

Dan said expressionlessly, "It could be I'm the man they're going to hang."

"Don't," said Hugh desperately. "Don't, Dan. He isn't worth that."

Alarm beginning to show in his face, Greenwood said hastily, "No. I don't know what you mean, but I ain't worth it. I'm just a pitiful homeless old man, trying to make my miserable way through life, trying to do my duty as I see it."

Dan said, "You forced this boy into bondage to you— or tried to—illegally."

Greenwood seemed to draw back into a shell of fright.

To Hugh, Dan said, "Anyone see you serving him?"

"Lots of people," said Hugh, "a tavern-keeper with a

red satin waistcoat with gold lace or something on it at a stage stand, a union stage stand, back west of here. A place with a flagpole in the road. I have an idea there is a man who will be anxious, and more than anxious, to testify against him."

Dan's face became a mask. In a rage so powerful that he could speak only in a whisper he said, "Greenwood, how would you like to go to jail?"

"I'd die in jail," said Greenwood simply. "I couldn't stand the fare. I ain't in the best of health."

Hugh suddenly felt that he was speaking the truth.

"If I ever," said Dan, "*ever* hear of another boy working for you—legally or otherwise—I'll see that you get just that. Death behind bars. All right, son, let's mount and get on."

Before he swung into the saddle, Hugh said, "Funny thing, Mr. Greenwood, I'm not even Joe Caffery, who was out of his state and not even owned by Mr. Gadsby, as far as that goes. I'm Hugh Perrine."

They mounted. Behind them, as they rode away, they left a shrunken old man, gaping, almost gibbering in terror.

At the eastern edge of town, they came to a crossroad and a fingerpost with wooden, arrow-pointed boards. One, pointing forward, said, "Cincinnati." Two others, pointing behind them said, "New Albany," "Corydon." A fourth, pointing at right angles to the north, said, "Corlock." They took this road to the north.

Corlock, though they got to it not long after, proved to be mainly shut in for the night and dark. A large segment of its hard-working denizens had already gone to bed, most of the others, likely, had gone to Deevers Ford for a little festivity.

The town actually seemed to be a string of tiny hamlets, three or four, perhaps, along one side of the road only and not quite joined to each other. The long ragged row of dark buildings, their lightless windows shiny black, their roofs pale yellow beneath the moon, seemed completely isolated, existing apart from the world of man. Hugh said as much to Dan but Dan shook his head.

"No," he said. "This is a prosperous and very busy little settlement. This short length of sorry road is actually an important link between the traffic of the north and the traffic of the east and west on the pike we just left. Through Corlock, connections are made between the river south of us and the Great Lakes to the north. It is also a funnel for many of the giant Conestoga freight wagons."

Here and there a light shone. They located an inn, stabled the horses, reserved lodgings for themselves, and set out in their search. In the first round, they decided, they would simply look for Caffery. No questions. Then, if they were unable to find him, they would try again, asking. Knowing Joe's deviousness, Hugh decided he might prefer it that way.

Was he in town? Was he in jail? Was he still alive?

When Hugh saw him, he almost passed him by. He was in an unexpected place, dressed in an unexpected way, doing unexpected things.

They were walking down the dirt path that served as a sidewalk, past a big brightly lighted window. On the glass in the center of the pane was painted a blue disc. Lettering below it said, "Blue Ball Stage Company." Beneath this, the printing said, "Forty miles of Line but a Million Miles of Schedules. Connections East, West, North, South: Anywhere in the World. *Office & Passenger Waiting Room*."

There were about fifteen people in the room, sitting on benches and chairs. Some were sleeping. All had luggage piled around their feet. Behind a counter was Joe Caffery, hardly recognizable in a young businessman's clothes: dead black suit, dead white shirt, neat black stock. Three or four people were standing before him, and he was talking to them, gesticulating, turning this way and that, taking papers from pigeonholes, restoring them, writing things down, shaking his head, frowning, smiling.

"He's working out schedules for them," Dan explained.

Hugh and Dan entered and pushed their way to the countertop.

"I want a ticket to Paris, France," said Hugh. "Fast express. By way of New York City and California. Would you please work out a schedule of connections for me?"

Caffery jerked his head around. Without moving a muscle of his face, he said, "Yes indeed, sir. That's what we're here for, to serve the public. Perhaps you'd like to stand outside the door in the nice fresh air until I can get around to it."

Hugh and Dan left the office and stood in the night on the sidewalk.

Ten minutes later, Joe Caffery joined them.

The two boys stood and beamed at each other.

"Joe," said Hugh. "This is Dan Nichols. He just saved me from an awful thing. He's all right. You can talk before him. Are you———?"

"I'm fine," said Caffery. "Never been better. How did you find me? If you can, others can."

Hugh told him about the stage driver and the patched cavalry boots. "I thought you were in bad trouble and peddling your clothes, or even worse—that other people were peddling them. So we looked you up," said Hugh.

"Joe, you're free!"

Together, Dan and Hugh explained it to him.

"You were free," said Dan, "the minute Gadsby led you over the state line."

At first Caffery looked angry; then he looked pleased and blew out his breath.

He said, "I reached this little town of Corlock, changed my name to Philip Lusterman, and got this job. I seem to have a sort of gift for the work. I'm gettin' along wonderful. And it's got a future."

"Then I guess you won't be changing your name back," said Hugh.

"No," said Caffery. "But not because I'm afraid to. For another reason entirely. I never much cared for Joe Caffery and his wicked companions. But I have only the highest admiration for that busy and honest young businessman, Mr. Philip Lusterman."

A woman came out of the waiting room and began to yell at Caffery. She was loaded down with luggage and had a sticky-faced baby under her arm. She put her face up to Caffery's and bellowed, "On my way to Natchez, how much extra will it cost me if I stop off and run over and see my sister at Joplin, Missouri?"

"Just step inside," said Caffery, "and we'll look it up. That's what we're here for, to serve the public."

He waved good-by to Hugh and Dan behind his back and ushered her back into the office.

Dan laughed. Even Hugh, despite himself, smiled a little.

They started to their inn.

X

THE INN at Corlock was actually a small group of buildings: a little grocery-office along the sidewalk, a big
square low-eaved log structure behind it, and a stable.
Dan led Hugh to the big log building and Hugh waited
while he knocked the coals from his pipe and extinguished
them carefully with his foot. There was a sogginess in
the night which Hugh interpreted as a forerunner to
rain and then probably a cold snap; November was on its
way.

Hugh had never seen an inn like this before and said
so. He thought of all the inns he had passed and how different they could be from one another, how different

the Merry Fifer was from the President Polk.

"This is the type referred to as a dormitory," said Dan. "Take a look inside."

There was a window a few feet away. Hugh stared through the pane. It was what he had always imagined an army barracks would look like. In the faint glow of the dim night light within, he could see rows of cots along the walls. Men were sleeping. Men were paring their toenails. Men were eating apples or sandwiches. Some of them were dressed, some were half dressed, and some were in their long underwear.

It looked pretty squalid to Hugh. "For men only, eh?" he said.

"Men only tonight, from the appearance of things," Dan said. "If women were present the males would be a little more decent in their attire. But many a backcountry congressman, his wife, and children, have passed the night in just such a place."

Dan suddenly bcame very grave.

"Hugh," he said quietly. "I've decided to close my season. I'm going home."

It was as though the world had come to an end for Hugh. It had seemed, somehow, that this was going to go on forever, throughout eternity: Dan, Hugh, and the three beautiful horses.

After a moment, when a little strength came back to him, Hugh began to argue, though he sensed beforehand that it would be of no use.

He said, "Why right now? Why so soon?"

"It's going to turn cold and rainy."

"We could hit for the deep south."

Dan shook his head.

"And what do you mean, home?" asked Hugh. "I kind of got the idea this was your home, you know, the horses and the pike."

"It's time for us to close up and head back, Hugh."

"Us?"

"Will you go with me?"

Hugh nodded. He was afraid to speak, afraid to say anything that might make Dan change his mind. Afraid even to ask, "Go back where?"

Dan explained. "I own a horse-breeding farm in Illinois, the Blue Ash. I breed Morgans and am doing pretty good. But I've got a restless nature, I guess, and for two months late in the summer I go on the road and try to work off a little of my excess energy. It helps my business too. It gets Blue Ash better known."

A horse farm, thought Hugh. Nothing but horses. What could be more wonderful?

"I'd like it," said Dan, "if you'd come and sort of help

around, if you can stand living with horses?"

"I love horses," said Hugh softly. "I'll do my very best. You'll never be sorry."

"I know I won't," said Dan. "Shall we go in and try to get a little sleep?"

The Author

Merle Constiner is one of the few people who can success-
fully combine a hobby with a career. He has been a writer
for many years, publishing regularly in many national maga-
zines. He has also pursued his interest in American history,
especially the stories of the more colorful and unconventional
early Americans—mendicants, journeymen, itinerant showmen, and tavern exhibitors. From years of research, he has
amassed a large collection of primary source material on the
period after the American Revolution and before the Civil
War. Mr. Constiner's hobby, therefore, contributes greatly to
the accuracy of his writing when he incorporates his knowl-
edge of early American life into the backgrounds of his
stories. In *Meeting at the Merry Fifer*, life along the roads
and trails of the Midwest in 1846 is accurately and warmly
portrayed.

Mr. Constiner lives in his birthplace, Monroe, Ohio, with
his wife Susannah.